THE HYPERMARKET

Gabriel García Ochoa

I0533808

ISBN: 978-0-578-65096-8

Printed in the United States of America

Published by LCG Media

Suggested Retail Price (SRP) $10.95

Edited by Jonathan Marcantoni

Cover and Design by Yanina Spizzirri

The Hypermarket is printed in Garamond

To Scott

Part 1:

The End of the Beginning

The Hypermarket

I entered the library with nothing but a pencil and the sixth volume of Sir Richard Francis Burton's *Arabian Nights*.

The Houghton Library at Harvard University houses an army of treasures. I visit it regularly for research. It is a beautiful place, a classic example of a rare-book library. Wood-panelled walls, oil paintings in the main reading room, a foyer with marble busts and a spiral staircase ascending to God knows where but leading down to the bathrooms. Some of the documents at the Houghton are simply priceless. As a historian, I feel nothing but reverence for them. Take the Dr Johnson collection for example (invaluable!); or that glorious eleventh century manuscript donated by the Walerians after they sold their castle in Cornwall, MS TYP 202, with an illustration of Bede the Venerable presenting Bishop Acca of Hexam with a book that he himself wrote–the Book of Judith from the *Vetus Latina*–an outstanding, early example of meta-drawing. I would take a bullet for many of these books; and yet, and yet…The impulse that drove me to temptation was unlike anything I had felt before. It went beyond the shy thrill I often experience in the presence of the Houghton's other jewels, that puerile and covetous knee-jerk reflex that dissipates when the mind steps in to stabilise the heart. But this was different.

This particular document was not held in high regard by the Library. It did not belong to any of its special collections. It had been erroneously catalogued, evidently, and some of its more fascinating features had escaped whomever had curated its entry. The monk Dondraluus of Abysynnia tells us time is a river that flows backwards. According to him, the future is what has already happened, but our restricted point of view does not allow us to differentiate it from the past. Nietzsche, of course, talks about the Eternal Return: time as an ever-spinning wheel, concentric circles with the blueprint of History playing over and over again. Claptrap, I used to say. Or, if one wished to show a more indulgent disposition, we might call these ideas *rudimentary philosophy*. At least that was my view until I came across the diary.

It was written in French, by a Spaniard. Ten or twenty pages into the text, the author had hand copied a letter. According to his commentary, embedded within this letter was a long passage found in a roll of vellum dating back to the seventh century, Anno Domini. Also a diary, to make things more confusing. That document was not the original either, but rather a first-hand translation of a papyrus that had once belonged to the collection of translated documents housed at none other than the Serapeum itself. The entry in the diary that spoke of the letter was dated 1816, the diarist a man by the strange name of Nándor Custos-Hora.

Normally, I would have ignored this sort of Babelic drivel. As anyone who has dabbled in translation knows, the practice really ought to be called *mistranslation*. The translator's essence, in spite of his professionalism and attempts at objectivity cannot help but contaminate the text; no one is hermetic. Meaning, as we know, is an elusive bird that not only nests in words but is made of them too. Translation is not that different from transmigration, and the translator becomes a vehicle for the reincarnation of the ideas of another. But the context for the new text is inevitably different, and meaning is contingent on context! This is in the case of a first translation based on the original, of course. When a document has been sieved by as many hands, tongues and centuries as this…well, I have no interest in such things. Or so I thought.

I sat down with the volume of Burton's *Nights* and my #2½ pencil. It took Mary, the librarian whom I have known for about fifteen years, less than five minutes to find the diary and bring it to me. She placed the item on the desk and I thought back to last Thursday when I first came across it. An unsettling feeling had taken hold of me early that morning after hearing on the radio that the singer Otis Redding had died in an airplane crash. I was in the kitchen, putting together a repast of lettuce and raw broccoli for Galland, my pet iguana. The news was followed by the announcement of this year's literary Nobel: a man by the name of Miguel Asturias. I may have heard Redding's name before; Asturias I knew nothing about. But the strongest *déjà vu* I have ever experienced ground me to a halt as I walked from the sink to the breakfast table. The sensation, like a bad aftertaste, stayed with me all morning. I went to the Houghton that Thursday afternoon hoping to cheer myself up. I already had a stack of other documents to get through when I came across the diary. I was about to skip it altogether, but the familiar curiosity that has driven my career gave me a shy shove in the ribs. I started leafing through and a line caught my eye:

The Hypermarket is big and sells almost everything.

That word, *Hypermarket*, made little sense to me. I kept reading:

The shelves in the aisles are stacked up so high you can't see the last one. Going from one section to another usually takes time, so it's important to plan your visit ahead. The last time my mother and I travelled from the Canned Vegetables section to the Meat section—a silly decision we made on the spot without thinking it through—we had to wait a full day for a ranger to show up and escort us. Apparently, the roads are no longer safe.

On our way to the Meat section I picked some flowers. There are parts of the Hypermarket where the linoleum floor gives way to moss and a young, tender turf. There are some—those who have travelled to Health and Cosmetics—who claim there are trees as tall as shelves there, thousands of years old, with things living in them. These are old wives' tales, like the story of the Time Witch, or the Elephant Man. No one even knows if the fabled Health and Cosmetics section really exists. I once saw a faun, though, prancing around aisle 202. His name was Saul.

There is a cemetery. Mum says we went there once when Father died, but I don't remember. I was very young and the cemetery is too far for me to go and explore on my own. Our village is by the lake, so we're not far from the Fish and Seafood section. It is a very small village though, a hamlet really. My aunt used to live with us until she married. Where she lives now is a real village. She and her husband are next to the Bakery section. My aunt has grown fat since she married, not because she's heavy with child or anything as tragic as that, she's just fat. Everyone who lives by the Bakery section is fat. She visits us every fortnight or so. When I hear the buzz of her motorized trolley I run out of the cottage in excitement. No one in our village owns a motorized trolley. Usually, the day after my aunt visits, when Mum and I walk down the main road we get looks (either of envy or admiration, I'm never sure) for having such a wealthy relative. I like it.

My aunt normally brings me something, wraps, or bagels or a baguette. I love them. When they're still inside the paper wrapping their smell makes my mouth water. There's nothing like biting into a crunchy bun: the first moment when your teeth, after considerable effort, break the outer layer and fight their way through the rest of the firm, nourishing mass. Mum says it's good exercise for the jaw. Sometimes, if we're lucky, Auntie will bring us a piece of aged bread too, the expensive kind, and we get to sample the bits of greenery that are considered a delicacy by those in the know, meaning the people who live next to the Bakery, like my aunt.

My aunt's husband is well-off. He doesn't work for the Bakery section, but he owns a small business that transports flour and other ingredients—yeast, salt— from the Baked Goods section on the other side of the hill, to the Bakery. He owns a fleet of five or six electric trolleys and I think he has a few of the manual ones too. No one really knows who works for the Bakery section, or any section for that matter. Hypermarket workers don't live with us. They pass on the product, sometimes give us information if they're in the mood, but that's all.

My father was a fisherman. His business was never as big as my uncle's but he used to catch for people who sold his fish to the Fish and Seafood section. Mum says he died in a very silly way, easily preventable and yet so common these days. We were on our way to get some eggs. The carton was down to two and we needed to stock up for the week. Mother says she told me that morning that just because I hadn't seen them, it didn't mean hens weren't real. Where else would the eggs come from? They just were, I told her. That would be like saying that fish from the Canned Fish section grew up in cans, Mum replied, and I had seen Father hurl them out of the lake and into the dingy with the net. That made sense. I don't, by the way, recall any of this conversation, but Mother has told me about it many, many times. So, my dad and I were walking through the woods on our way to get some eggs, Mum had straggled for some reason. And then it happened: an entire box of canned dog food fell from the sky. The fog was thick that day, CloudMan was probably doing some mischief up there, so Mum couldn't even tell what shelf it came from. Apparently, the box hadn't been stacked properly. My father died instantly. A can hit me on the head, on my right side, and I have forgotten many things since.

Sometimes, Mother gets really sad with memories of Father and starts to cry. If Aunt is visiting she'll say that Father would have been proud to know he died the way he lived: doggy style. I don't understand what that means, but Mother laughs until her tears dry out, and then some more. I like to see Mum happy like that. Aunt then brings the spinning wheel out of the closet. The two of them cackle and hug each other for a while, then start working on their yarn. They can spin for hours.

Three weeks ago, a rack collapsed. One of its shelves started to buckle, gave in, and then the whole thing came down. Seven people died. I wasn't there, but our next-door neighbour—I always forget her name—saw it happen. She is a tall lady, short white hair, always wears a purple robe, with a golden medallion dangling from her neck. She's the one who suggested I start writing a diary to remember things. Anyway, Mother says we live in perpetual fear that something like this could one day signal the beginning of the end, that one day a rack will fall sideways and push another, and another, and another, until the entire World comes crashing down...

Mother and I live on the pension she receives from the Pet Food section for Father's accident. She says what we're left with after Inter-Section taxes is a pittance. *Twenty-five per cent of our pension is taken by the Cashiers. They say it is being turned into Food Stamps under Mother's name, which she'll be able to collect when she turns sixty. She says we'll never see a single stamp.*

Mother works too. She stitches the hems of tea towels that are delivered to our home every day. Hundreds and hundreds of them. We don't even know what Section they're for. She's been doing it for years. At one point Mother thought about sewing her own things, little garments maybe, to sell here and there. She decided against it in the end. It is very unlikely the Cashiers will find out, but if they do, you are in trouble.

The Cashiers normally travel in groups. They are assigned to different areas of the Hypermarket, on rotation. Old stories say they were once stationary, that they lived in little houses at the end of the world, all lined up like jars of pickled vegetables. They had human heads, not half-bull like now, and after visiting a Section you would walk up to a Cashier and pay your taxes. As if you could walk up to a Cashier without fear freezing your legs! Like the Health and Cosmetics tales, these are the kind of stories that talk about cards of credit, the Time Witch, men with the power to release the hidden forces in the atom, poisoned baked apples and coffee shops with mermaid flags. CloudMan, who lives in the skies and looks after the winds, the Lady who became a Tree and then went back to being a Lady, and even the Great War between the Elephant Man's forces and the Holy House of the Charging Bull, they all belong to the same mythology, the Book of Tales that Never Happened. They're good stories, though.

The Cashiers' uniforms are black, with a wide, white circle on the front of their shirts. Inside the circle, there is the coat of arms of the Holy House of the Charging Bull. That's all they wear. They carry long knives, thirty centimetres or so, made of rat thighbone. They patrol different sections of the Hypermarket in the name of Peace and the Law of the Plutocrat-Apostle, but they are usually the ones disturbing both. Unless we owe them money we stay away from the Cashiers.

The Hypermarket knows what we take. I don't know how it does, but it does. Mother says there are a thousand eyes watching in the hooting of the owl and the sweeping of the mop. So we all pay our debts. That's what the Cashiers are there for: to collect what we owe, in the name of the Holy House of the Charging Bull. Sooner or later the Cashier will get you. Most of us pay them back willingly, but there are some who don't. There are those who take from the Hypermarket without giving in return, Insolvents, whose actions threaten the very fabric of our society, Mother says. Thankfully they are a small group, so small they have almost disappeared. When the Cashiers find an Insolvent you better run fast or look the other way.

Mother and I left the village today to see Aunt. She was supposed to visit us no later than a quadrant of the sundial. She is very punctual, so after an hour's wait, Mother said something must have happened to her.

We left the village, wrapping ourselves in our shawls against the biting Aircon from the North. I feared the worst. I kept thinking we would come across my aunt's abandoned trolley on our way to her village. A few weeks ago, as we were getting ready for bed, Mother and I heard a pack of rats howling in the distance. I'd never heard that horrid wail before. It made my heart beat fast. If Aunt had been attacked by a pack of hungry rats her trolley would still be there, by the side of the aisle, probably. But what if she had chanced upon a band of Insolvents, their nature much more vicious than the rats'? They would have killed her and taken her trolley too! Oh, poor Aunt.

We walked as fast as we could. The aisle to the Bakery Section is a wide one, so wide that you can scarcely see the shelves on either side. It wasn't well lit today. The turf was still wet, as though covered in morning dew, unusual for the hour. Mother was very quiet on our way there. In fact, she didn't say a word. I wanted to make her feel better but had no idea what to say, so I kept quiet.

The distance to Aunt's village seemed longer than ever. I pictured every metre we walked divided into centimetres, each centimetre halved and halved again, and again, and again, until Mother and I were lost in that small infinity, unable to reach my aunt's house, choked by our own anguish and misery. I was wrong, of course. We did eventually reach Auntie's village. When we did I wished we had gotten lost in my imaginary abyss.

We saw the smoke even before we got to the top of the hill. Mother and I started to run. The sprinkler system was on, but in spite of the heavy rain falling over Aunt's village, the fires roared. Maybe the sprinklers had gone off in other parts of the aisle too, and that was why the turf was wet? I wish I hadn't seen Mother's expression. Oh, I can't even describe it! She took off, running down the hill. I followed her, tried to tell her to stop and wait for me, and

And that is where the copied excerpt of the letter comes to an end. I read the rest of the diary in less than a week. There were no other examples of the letter anywhere else in the document, and no discussion of it either, aside from a single sentence where the author calls it 'a charming tale, fit for the nursery.'

Normally, I would have hand copied it—that is what a researcher does, of course. That is what I have always done. But I could not help myself! Mary the librarian never suspected a thing. No one did. I carefully ripped out the flimsy pages and placed them inside the *Arabian Nights*, where they disappeared like leaves in a forest.

Volume six of the *Nights* has rejoined its brethren in my study. I have not opened it since that last visit to Harvard. Out of guilt, I have not been able to visit the Houghton since either, which breaks my heart. The volume manifests itself in my dreams, the stolen trove it keeps is persistently, disturbingly constant in my mind. I know that if I open volume six on the 602nd Night, the most magical of nights, the inserted pages will be waiting for me, a testament to my shame, but more importantly, a challenge to the weak scaffolding of my reality. That time is an illusion, or rather, an example of the myriad variations of *times* that stretch and overlap, contorting and spinning back upon themselves without us ever noticing the difference, is a horror I do not care to entertain. And yet, and yet…Today, I sit in my study gazing at the bookshelf that houses volume six of the *Nights*, and I cannot help but wonder whether the events I write about have already happened, or are about to.

Apollo and Daphne

I looked at her from inside her father's old T2 Kombi van, mesmerized. I couldn't believe what Laurel was doing. I was in the driver's seat, parked, my hand out the window, stubbornly trying to scratch the flaking blue paint off the door of the van to reveal the rust when Laurel walked up to the fenced rodeo ring, put her hands on one of the rails, and propped herself up. She was inside, with the bull.

There was no one around, or at least I couldn't see anyone. Cloncurry—the Curry—is a small town in North West Queensland. Once you leave the town proper you can drive for miles and miles without sighting a soul. Even if you are *in* the Curry, less than three thousand people live there. If most of the town is gathered on one end and you happen to be on the other you feel like the last person on Earth. There was nothing going on that Sunday, but it was a Sunday, and it is the Curry. I parked outside the Equestrian Centre, like Laurel told me to, and was not surprised to find it deserted. Except for the bull. What the hell was that lonely bull doing there, and what did Laurel want with it?

At first, the bull paid no attention to her. Laurel had her back to the red, white, and blue rails of the fence surrounding the ring. She was slightly bent forward. Her legs moved sideways, opening and closing along the perimeter of the rodeo, like a crab ready to fight.

By the time I saw this I had left the Kombi and found my way to the tiered seats that surround the ring like an amphitheatre. The Equestrian Centre is brand new. It was donated by the Oostanens, a rich, Dutch-Australian family who had invested heavily in cattle and arable land. Whispers here and there suggested the Oostanens were doing illegal experiments on their cattle, to improve the quality of their beef. The Centre usually plays host to the Curry's events, rodeos most of them.

We had been here a couple of times. Once, during a rodeo show, I sprang to my feet when a poor bastard was thrown off his buckjumper; Laurel's dad laughed and pulled me back to my seat, Laurel giggled too. I stared at the fallen rider, half-covered in sand like a crumbed fish fillet, and not knowing what else to do I waved my arms, dumbfounded, just as I was now doing with my girlfriend. I gestured at Laurel, waved frantically to catch her attention, but it didn't work. All her attention was focused on the bull. I thought about shouting, telling her to get out. I didn't. I couldn't. I stood there stupidly, flapping my arms.

I think the bull had already noticed her but it kept staring at the ground. Its tail flicked. Maybe the bull was assessing the situation, trying to figure out Laurel's intentions? That made two of us.

Less than half an hour ago Laurel and I had hopped inside her father's rusty, red and blue van to go for a drive. We were having a perfectly normal conversation about her parents and the grazing station, and how excited her mother was that we were visiting for the long weekend. The sky was the intense cornflower blue you can only get in the middle of spring on a cloudless afternoon in North Queensland. Laurel studies rivers. Well, one river. Her background is in geography, she wrote her master's thesis in potamology, and now she is specialising in the irrigation patterns of the Cloncurry, which have been affecting her Dad's cattle since she was like five years old. I turned down the radio to better hear what Laurel was saying, then she asked me to stop the van. She stepped out and walked directly to the rodeo ring. And now we're here.

The bull was keeping its head low. It looked docile despite its bulk. Laurel's father raises Brahman bulls, the 'cattle of the Sun God'. This one looked like a Brahman, except bigger, much bigger, more like the Sun God himself. Brahman bulls, at least the ones Laurel's father raises, are not aggressive. They don't have horns either. Which clearly meant the animal in the enclosure was not a Brahman bull. To say this bull had horns, casually, just like that, like you were talking about a rainy afternoon or a good coffee (Oh, look! The bull has horns…) would be an understatement. Its horns were obscene. Minarets that curled, thick at the base, slimmer and slimmer as they twisted their way up to the middle blade of a shining trishula.

Laurel was not herself. I hope that has become pretty obvious by now. Even though she grew up in a grazing station, it's not like she's in the habit of jumping into rodeos with unknown bulls. Her long, unwashed hair had fallen on her face, strands of it curved into her mouth. She was wearing denim overalls, which she usually wears when she works at the river, and a short-sleeved green shirt. When she's dressed like that she reminds me of Scout Jean from *To Kill a Mockingbird*, a grown-up version of Scout: beautiful, masculine and feminine all at once. The sun must have been just past its zenith because I could see only the slightest hint of Laurel's and the bull's shadows. I gestured to her once more, and again, she ignored me.

I had a vision of the bull raising its head, locking Laurel with its gaze, the ends of its horns the sight of a sniper's rifle. *Charge!* Its entire body, two thousand pounds turned into a red bullet aimed directly at Laurel. Bull, bullet. Of course, that didn't happen. It was my Bugs Bunniesque imagination. To my credit though, given what had happened in the last five minutes—and more importantly, what was *about* to happen!—it wouldn't have been entirely out of line.

Laurel kept circling the circumference of the rodeo, moving closer to the bull until they were only three or four metres away from each other. Once the mirage of distance evaporated and they were close enough, I understood the animal's size. My stomach, the back of my knees and my hamstrings, went cold.

Laurel took a step forward and the bull finally raised its head. Its legs scraped the ground. Bulls actually do that? They do, and they move their heads from side to side too in a universal body language that says, rather eloquently, *I'm warning you, don't mess with me, stay away.*

Clearly, Laurel did not speak Bull. Or if she did she was just ballsier than I could ever be. Probably both. At any rate, she stood her ground. I think that was the right moment to say something, to scream at her, tell her to get out. But I didn't. I was too scared. I thought that if I shouted I would break whatever spell was keeping my girlfriend safe, or that she would lose her concentration, look at me, and at that moment be gored to death. I wasn't thinking straight. I was rooted to the spot with only stupid ideas running through my head and my phone in my hand.

Why was my phone in my hand? I had no idea. When did I get it out? I didn't know, but since it was out I thought about calling her father. And how, in the name of God, would that help? Well, maybe he could come here and do something. Laurel's parents' place wasn't far. And Johnny raises bulls for a living. A quick drive down the road, twenty minutes at most. He drives like a madman too. He'd be here in ten. And then what? Face the bull himself? A seventy-year-old man? What was Johnny going to do that I couldn't do right now? I called him. I was out of ideas. I tried twice but he didn't pick up. Then the bull charged.

Its name was Phoebus. I didn't find this out until later, when the whole thing was over, later, when I walked Johnny back to his car, still shocked, and saw a sign swinging from a horizontal pole on one of the cattle trucks behind the ring, the kind of sign you'd expect to see outside a saloon in a bad Western, hinged to a crossbeam or a ceiling, a ridiculously hyperbolic sign in white letters and capitals: PHOEBUS.

I dropped my phone. It fell between the seat in front and the row where I stood. The bull wasn't far from Laurel, only a couple of metres away. I don't know how she managed to avoid the charge or why Phoebus didn't simply alter its trajectory to gore her. Perhaps once bulls charge they can't change their minds? She twirled once, a Sufi dancer warming up. Then I was on my knees, stupidly, frantically trying to recover my phone, hoping Johnny wouldn't call back.

It took me a couple of seconds to find it. I stood up and looked at the rodeo rings again. I saw the bull thrash its horns in defiance. Laurel had locked eyes with it. This time they were probably ten metres apart. And behind them? What was going on behind them, on the other side of the rodeo ring? It lasted two heartbeats, but I saw a woman, almost certainly a vagrant, rushing away. She had short white hair, a walking stick in each hand, and strangest of all, she was topless. Her bare, white breasts flopped with only a necklace, or a medallion between them. Then the gravity of the present pulled me back to Laurel.

The same scene unfolded, only the distance and the angle

had changed. Before, I had seen the bull charge at Laurel from south to north, from my side of the ring to hers. Now it was coming from the opposite direction, the bull charging at both of us, so to speak. The outcome was slightly different too: this time, as Laurel twirled, the bull's left flank hit her. She fell and I squealed as though someone had bashed the small of my back with a lead pipe.

Back home in Melbourne Laurel and I like going to the Botanical Gardens near our apartment. If the weather is nice and we don't have much planned we'll take a blanket, a bottle of wine. We'll laze around by the foot of a huge tree not far from the Yarra River. Sometimes I go there by myself, to think of Laurel if she's visiting her parents, or to write. I came up with the entire first draft of *The Language of Flowers*, my first play, under that tree. But I'm mostly there with Laurel. There is a small bronze plaque on the trunk of the tree that says it's a Montezuma Cypress. It would probably take ten adults holding hands to circle the cypress. On one of our first visits to the tree, a late morning in early spring, we were making our way through the gardens to reach the riverside. You need to

walk down a set of steep stone steps–probably thirty or so–
to get to the tree. The descending steps curve around a rock
wall to the right and there is a metal railing on the left that
almost shivers if you put a hand on it. I was walking behind
Laurel with our picnic blanket under my arm and a couple of
books in my hands. The steps are mossy at the best of times
and that morning I obviously misjudged just how slimy they
were. I slipped. Surprisingly, I didn't fall. I remember how tak-
en aback I was by my reaction. My hand shot left to hold on to
the railing, which convulsed violently, but held. The speed and
accuracy of my hand surprised me. If it hadn't been for that
automatic response I would have fallen down a pretty steep
flight of steps, if not to my death, then to a whole lot of pain,
taking Laurel down with me. But my trusty hand stepped up
to the challenge. What incredible machines our brains are. In a
fraction of a second mine was able to determine the distance
between me and the railing, decide that the books and blanket
I carried needed to be dropped; it understood the necessary
speed at which my arm had to move in order to grip the railing
in time, the right strength to stop myself from falling, all with-

out the need of a single conscious thought on my part.

What I was about to do was similar. It felt like a knee-jerk reflex in the sense that it was entirely out of my control. The kind of thing your brain does to save you, and yet, in this case, by doing so it put me in more danger. It sounds counterintuitive, doesn't it? Maybe neither my brain nor my body needed to be saved that afternoon. Perhaps it was my soul running toward salvation because, had I not done what I did, I don't think I would have been able to live with myself.

I jumped inside the rodeo ring and started screaming, maniacally. I was facing the bull, which must have thought, with good reason, that all humans are deranged. The animal seemed confused. It stared at me incredulously, if there can be such a thing as taurine incredulity.

I saw Laurel's face. She was smiling. I'd never seen that smile on her. Great joy, perfect happiness. Was she happy because I had jumped in? Was this her plan, to drag me into the rodeo ring? A test, maybe? While I was asking myself these questions, the bull's allotted time for philosophical ponderings (half a second) was over and he was back to basics. I was the new intruder in his ring and charging at me was not in breach of etiquette. I had neither Laurel's grace nor courage. The moment I saw the animal move in my direction I scrambled for the fence. I jumped. My twenty-eight-year-old, slim but adrenaline-fuelled body, managed. I grabbed hold of the top railing and lifted myself to the other side. I ran back to the stalls. I looked at my phone. Johnny had tried to call me while this was going on, twice, but I obviously didn't notice my phone ringing. Somehow, miraculously, it was still in my pocket.

The bull looked tired. It trotted towards a side of the ring, bored, it seemed, and at least for now, not caring about Laurel. Phoebus lowered its head like a hound catching a scent, or like a grazing bull, perhaps a better image because, well, Phoebus was a bull. It was no longer facing my girlfriend. It stood eight or nine metres away, as though trying to make up its mind on what to do next.

I waved my arms. Laurel! I screamed. She stopped staring at the bull. She looked up and smiled at me again.

The moment lasted two seconds. Her eyes went back to the bull. Phoebus paced a narrow circle and repositioned itself.

Laurel and the bull were separated by a good ten metres, facing each other. The bull stomped its front hooves, right, left, two, then three times. When it finally lowered its head and took off, Laurel stood her ground. She bent her knees ever so slightly, like a basketball player playing defence, her torso bent at a sixty-degree angle.

I thought she was going to spin again. I thought she was going to do her dervish thing and be safe. But she didn't move. She still wasn't moving. The bull charged. It was going too fast. Phoebus lowered its neck ready to scoop her off the ground. I went cold. I couldn't move. I was as paralysed as Laurel. I couldn't will the scream inside me to make its way to my mouth. The scene must have taken less than five seconds but I saw it unfold in slow motion. The left horn askew positioned for the gore, ten centimetres away…less, the length of a packet of cigarettes.

Then it happened. Perhaps I willed it, or maybe I lost my mind with grief. I like to believe Laurel was a magical being all along and that's why I fell in love with her in the first place. Her dirt-streaked Nikes were the first thing to go. They burst open like ripe pomegranates. The skin I had kissed by the river under the shade of our tree, naturally white but tanned after months of working under the touch of the sun, grew dark and darker still. As though Laurel had been tumbling in the grass all afternoon, leaves and small flowers bloomed from her hair. Roots burrowed into the ground out of toes and fingers. The speed of the metamorphosis was inconceivable: a nature documentary fast-forwarded to show a catalogue of seasons in a second. The bull bellowed as its left horn hit the trunk and splintered. The cypress of our most tender moments stood inside the rodeo ring. The enclosure could barely contain it. Laurel was not bleeding from the lower left side of her torso, she was not screaming; that image had been summoned by my treacherous imagination. The *bull* was the one bawling and sobbing for its broken horn, in what sounded, eerily, like a woman's voice. The tree kept growing and growing until there was little room left for Phoebus.

The Language of Flowers

I

This morning I brought my son to 'The Castle'. 'Tis a museum, not a castle, but that's what he calls it. When I call it 'the museum' it's because I want him to learn the proper words. My son goes red in the face, holds his silver crayon over his head and yells over and over and over, castle, castle, castle! After a year and a half, me and my wife gave up and now we call it 'The Castle'.

My son's four. We don't know what's wrong with him. Doctors can't tell us. He doesn't look us in the eye and when he does it's like a mistake, like he didn't mean to, like me and my wife we were just standing there when his eyes moved past and saw us. He complains about his fingernails. He says they itch. He says he has to rub 'em to stop the tingles. Sometimes I see him next to the wall, pressing the side of his thumb to the cement, rubbing.

My wife's a nurse. On Sunday mornings, if she's not in the hospital she brings our son to the museum. Her other job is at *Olga's* waiting tables. 'Tis a diner near our apartment. 'Tis not open for breakfast so on Sunday mornings she brings the boy to the museum.

We are here, 'The Castle', me and my son. 'Tis a Sunday afternoon. As I said before, it ain't a castle. The mayor says our city has one of the best museums in the world. This is it, he says. The outside looks a bit like a castle, I guess, with the big columns and all.

I see him walking 'round the museum and 'tis hard to believe he ain't a normal boy. He walks 'cross the marble floor with his skinny legs. When the big rooms are empty it gets so quiet you can drop a pin and your deaf Pops will hear it fall. But when my boy walks you can't hear his steps, little echoes they are. He's really small. He stands in front of each painting.

We can't do more than one big room when we're here. He takes *ages*. I imagine he soaks up the details. If he was older I'd be telling everyone this is his thing, his *calling*, he wants to be a painter when he grows up.

Today's the first time we see 'The Dutch Masters'. Didn't even know we'd Dutch Masters. My son's wearing the same clothes he wears every time we're here. Jeans, red hoodie, blue tee with a smiling train in a circle. He's holdin' his silver crayon in his left hand. For months we've gone to the Japanese rooms. Never been to the Dutch Masters before. My son loves, what ya call 'em? Routes? Routines? Retinues? When he likes Japan it'll be silk screens and chopsticks for donkeys' years, in the same order, every time we are here. If he doesn't see 'em in the same order he'll get fidgety. He never cries, tho.

I didn't go to museums when I was a boy. Only when school took us there. I liked theatre, but we never had the dough to go. Grams used to take me on my birthdays after Pops passed. We watched *Peter Pan* like five times. My son steps in front of some touristy people. I can't see him. Now I can. He stands right in the middle of the tourists holding on to that silver crayon for dear life. Where I stand I can't see the painting he's looking at. I can only see the top right corner of the frame, part of the shiny rectangle with the names and stuff: *Jacob Cornelisz van Oostsanenm, Saul and the Witch of Endor. c.1526.*

The tourists move away. My son stays where he is. I take two steps, put my arm 'round his back. He's like a grass stem, a dandelion, thoughts floating in the wind. Flying away. I imagine him in a flowerpot. Growing and smiling ev'ry day. I'd learn to speak like a flower to talk to him. Is that bad? To think about him like that? Maybe I'm the dandelion. Maybe *my* brains are scattered in the wind.

Now I can see it. I think I like *Saul and the Witch of Endor*. There're two dudes in the middle of the painting, standing, both with goat's legs. An owl, a naked chick in her teens riding a flying skull pulled by two roosters, which is kinda hot, in a weird way. A woman, much older than the naked chick, a grandmother's at the centre of the painting, smack bang in the middle. Maybe she's the witch? She has a purple sheet wrapped 'round her waist, like a skirt, but doesn't cover her boobs. There's a golden medallion between them floppy boobs, with a very clear image of an elephant. In front of the witch, there's a horse with things coming out of its head, like an octopus crawling from its brains. I don't know what any of this shit means, but I like it. What does my little boy see when he looks at it? I cuddle his neck, play with his hair. I don't ask him what he thinks. Maybe we should give him a different haircut? The basin doesn't work. Too perfect. Unreal. He looks like a doll. He would hate that, tho, a different haircut.

I stare at the painting again. I squint. Looks like something's moving in the background. That's weird. A reflection in the glass, but I turn and there's nothing behind me. A trick? Like those old postcards with dolphins and hearts, hiding, and you can only see 'em with your eyes half closed? If it is, them Dutch boys were clever. I think I see a bird. There's light in the corners of the painting. Light with wings. Is it coming from behind the painting? Like, from the wall? The colours are softer. The painting's shining, so much. There's so much light *Saúl and the Witch of Endor* disappear.

There's nothing in the frame now. 'Tis transparent, like a window. Like glass. A bit dirty but I can see through it. There's a building. Lots of fog. What's happening? It takes me about ten seconds to recognize my hometown. That's the theatre. I'm standing in front of the theatre with my Grams. We're about to watch *Peter Pan*. How old? I'm eight? Ten? A cold morning but I'm excited. I've never been this excited…

The theatre disappears. Now the painting's a mirror, not a window. I see me in it. Not younger me like before, but me of today. Is it really me? I've never had a jacket like that, brown, so soft. A red scarf? I don't wear scarves. Why am I smiling? That ain't my smile but 'tis on my lips. Who are you? I want to know. But the me in the painting is walking away and I'm walking too. I feel my son's hand pulling, his body sliding to the left, walking to the next painting…

II

Michael could not understand Claire's words. Her voice came from Alastair's room, but it was distorted. Michael had the radio on trying to catch the last of the morning news before heading out. He put on the camel-hair jacket Claire had chosen for him, draped a scarf around his neck, and left the bedroom to join Claire and Alastair.

The two were already waiting by the front door. Alastair clutching the silver lighter, Claire holding Alastair's hand. If they left the apartment now, Michael thought, like this, with him leading the way, Claire's hand in his and Alastair's in Claire's, they would be like a family of elephants herding through the savannah, trunk to tail, tail to trunk.

Do you want to walk or take a taxi? Michael asked.

It's been cold, Claire said, let's take a cab.

The concierge hailed a taxi for them. Good idea, thought Michael, when he felt the hot air inside the taxi, too warm but comforting, bearable for a few minutes until they made it to the museum. When he was in town and not working on a matinee, Michael enjoyed spending time with Claire and Alastair. At the moment he found himself between jobs. His last play finished almost a month ago. The company spent two weeks filming a DVD of the show (marketing claimed it was 'live', but it wasn't; they hired a 'live' audience for the recording). Rehearsals for the new play Michael was starring in, *The Lan-*

guage of Flowers, did not start for another three weeks, but the last two weekends had been busy with interviews and commitments, and he had not been able to spend time with his family.

Claire had wanted to come to the museum. She did this with Alastair almost every weekend, and yet, here she was, sitting next to Alastair, holding his hand, ready to revisit two hours of kimonos, hand fans, silk prints, and enameled ebony chopsticks. The hand fans in particular had become Alastair's latest fixation. But Michael wasn't surprised. Claire was a saint. *No one* is a saint, thought Michael, not really, except Claire. She could have been a social worker, or a nurse or something. Honestly, she had the vocation for it.

Michael looked out the window. They were driving past *Olga's*, a Ukrainian restaurant they used to go to when Alastair was younger. It had a kid's section at the back with a big play set, a castle Alastair loved to climb. He called the restaurant 'The Castle'. For a moment, while they drove past Olga's, Claire was in the restaurant, a ghostly reflection superposed on the car window. She wore a short trench coat, black, double-breasted, fastened with a black belt. What was she wearing underneath?

A blouse? A warm, fawny sweater that matched Michael's jacket? Michael had no idea. He knew her pants were black, and she had tucked them inside her knee-high boots. Maybe we could have a bite at *Olga's* after the museum? he asked.

Claire's reflection on the window took its time to answer. The lips moved, mild cerise, but said nothing. She curled one of Alastair's locks around her index finger, a strawberry blond loop, same colour as her own hair before she started dyeing out the 'grey invaders', as she called them. Let's see, she said, looking at Michael. No smile. Two blinks.

When they arrived at the museum, to Michael's surprise, they did not walk straight to the Japanese Art permanent exhibition. They did head in that direction, but when they reached the threshold to 'Asian Art' Alastair smiled at his mother and walked away. The school therapist had said this sort of behaviour was positive and ought to be encouraged. Alastair had a mild case of autism; kids like him find it sometimes difficult to stray from patterns. Habits bring them certainty. What Alastair was doing, actively choosing to go somewhere new, was brave of him.

They walked past a painting of a seamstress, a Van Gogh apparently, but it looked nothing like the Van Goghs Michael had seen in Amsterdam. When his son stopped moving and it was clear they weren't going anywhere, Michael read the plaque on the wall. Cornelisz van Oostanen. Never heard of him, he thought.

Alastair stood before the painting clutching his lighter. The lighter, of course, had no gas. It was a trinket Alastair had found in a box or a drawer when they were moving houses. The lighter was silver, rectangular, with hard corners. It had a curious engraving in the middle: a circle with the front-facing head of a bull inside. The bull's horns twisted upward and outward to join the circle enclosing them. For some reason, Alastair had become attached to it, like a safety blanket. He took it everywhere and was very careful with it. As he clutched the lighter, Alastair didn't seem to be looking at the painting before him. He simply stood in front of it and stared. His eyes seemed to travel past the wall, into the distance. For all Michael knew they could be atop Mont Fort in Verbier, admiring the wintry landscape.

Claire opened her handbag, brought out a box of breath mints and offered one to Michael. I need the restroom, she said. The box closed with a metallic echo and was buried again in her handbag. Can you look after him for a second?

The *clicks* of Claire's high-heeled, knee-high boots became fainter and fainter. The museum was rather empty. There was a group of Spanish-speaking tourists standing one or two metres away from Alastair and Michael. They clustered around the Van Gogh of the seamstress taking photographs. Had Michael been there by himself, trying to contemplate van Oostanen's painting, he would have been distracted by them, annoyed. But his son was not concerned with them. Michael took a step forward and placed his arm across Alastair's back, resting his hand on the boy's shoulder. He kissed the crown of his head with lightness. Yesterday Claire had booked the hairdresser to come to the apartment and give Michael a cut. It was slightly different from the one he had before. Less symmetrical, thought Michael. It suits him.

A line from the new play came to mind, nosediving, for Michael's lips: *Maybe we should give him a different haircut?* It was a whisper, and no one took notice.

The new play he was starring in came about accidentally. Blake, Michael's manager, stumbled across the unknown Australian author at a writers' workshop. It's about a struggling family with a sick child. Both parents work two jobs. The mother can scarcely spend time with her son. The kid has autism, which is still the niche of a handful of specialists. His parents take him from doctor to doctor but no one can tell them what's wrong and money is pretty tight. It's a one-man show and Michael's character, the father, struggles to make sense of the situation.

The din died off as the Spanish-speaking group moved down the gallery. Michael and Alastair stayed moored. *Saul and the Witch of Endor. c.1526.* Michael had come to realise one of the many advantages of Alastair's condition was a different pace to life. Nuance. Before Alie, Michael had enjoyed going to museums, but to be honest he visited them like he visited a video store or the supermarket. He floated around, vaguely, skimmed here and there until something caught his attention. He read a name, a year, perhaps a country or the title of a piece that he knew he would forget in a minute or two. Alie taught him how to observe things, places. It wasn't so different from studying people when he was in acting school, but he had never done it with stuff, not with that intensity.

This was an interesting painting. Michael did not know who Saul was – a biblical character, surely – nor what his dealings with the Witch of Endor had been about, but he didn't have to. There were ruins in the middle of the scene that separated background and foreground, a broken Roman aqueduct, or perhaps an arch. You could see mayhem in the distance: ships tried to anchor but blustering winds kept them at bay, the dead rising, guards rushing down a street to deal with the rabble. There is a man with the head of an elephant, bleeding, and a woman sprouting roots from her legs. In front of the arch, there was a strange gathering: a faun and a satyr; three young women and a crone huddled around a horse with tentacles growing out of its head. Two owls peeked out from inside the robe of the main figure in the painting, the Witch of Endor, no doubt. Her face is angular, very strong features. Pointy chin and pointy ears, short white hair, black almond eyes with a triangular scar above the left eyebrow. The Witch held a wand in each hand: the first pointed to the ground, the second to the sky. Her chest was bare except for a medallion. She read out of a book with runes and other symbols. One final character flew above the gathering, a naked woman riding a skull pulled by two roosters. The rest of the composition left Michael unperturbed, the Witch included, but that lonely woman flying through the air, her nakedness, the mundane roosters raised to the level of evil sprites that pulled her skull chariot...he felt sad, slightly cold.

As a four-year-old boy, Michael would have been scared by a painting like this, but Alastair was fine. He must read them differently, Michael thought. A language of lines and symmetry rather than narrative. A language of flowers? he muttered. He smiled, thinking about the play again. Perhaps. I don't know.

Claire should be back by now, shouldn't she? Michael observed the painting again. Would his character ever look at a painting, he wondered? He didn't know. Did he go to museums? Could he afford to, time-wise, money-wise, which amounted to the same? Bus or subway? Michael hadn't seen the costumes.

What did he wear to the museum? I need to find out.

He imagined what his character would look like standing here with his son. Basic white tee, old leather jacket, jeans. Fonzie from *Happy Days* came to mind. No, no, no, different register. Maybe just visually. Older though. Tired, happy. A little worried? Van Oostsanen's painting seemed reflective and translucent, a transparent mirror. Where did Michael's imagination travel to, to summon this man? It took off, like a bird, and brought him back. And there he was, standing right in front of him. What do we have in common, you and I, aside from Alastair? What is your story?

Michael tried to picture Claire as a nurse and waitress. Her poise, her bearing, the three-hundred-dollar haircut. His mental image of his wife resisted but in the end, it proved pliable, as Claire would under the right circumstances. We bend or we break, and Claire would not break, he thought. He wanted to question his character. There wasn't much of a backstory in the script. What brought you here? Do you like the theatre, like me? How did you come by this life? He did not want to probe too much; that usually scared his characters away. Give him a couple of lines. It may help. He's not plausible yet, but it's only a first draft. Let it come. That'll do for now.

He caressed Alastair's shoulder and waited. Beyond the Witch of Endor and her fading retinue, the man in the mirror looked back at him. There was longing in his eyes, which were Michael's eyes too. He felt a soft tug on his arm. Claire was behind them, and Alie started walking to her.

CloudMan # 5,525

Hello,

My name is Gasparian. I don't think we've met. Or if we have I can't recall. I'm very sorry.

I started writing this because I didn't know what else to do with the paper and pen I found. I don't know if you exist, but I like to think you do. When I finish writing this letter I am going to fold it, over and over until I turn it into a paper boat. I will take out one of the bricks on my wall and let it sail to you. I hope you get it.

I must live in the present. There is much I don't remember. I know what I did last week, and the week before that, true, but my memory stops there. I am sorry, I wish I knew more. I feel light but empty. I know my name is Gasparian Nebula and that I am in charge of the East Wind clouds, and the Khrónoloop. That knowledge brings me comfort.

The wind reaches my tower from the West. I imagine a great Moose, his breath puffing gray mist, sending it my way. What do *you* imagine when you imagine things? What exists outside your tower? I like to look at the sky when it's clear. I close my eyes and imagine I am the sky. Calm, big. I don't dislike it here. I don't feel trapped. I am here and I do what I do.

Clouding takes most of my time. I work alone in the basement. There is charcoal everywhere. It makes it difficult, especially for the young clouds. They need to be clean when they leave the tower. But with a layer of soot staining my overalls, my face, and the tips of my fingers, it isn't always possible. There is no water to wash myself. Only tall, thick rolls of fabric, taller than me, leaning against a wall in the corner of the basement. I use that fabric to make the clouds, and every now and again to wipe my hands clean. The rolls are replaced every evening. The Time Witch replaces them. Last week I couldn't sleep and I walked down to the basement. I saw her there, dressed in purple. She smiled at me and moved the rolls around. I think she is mostly here for the Khrónoloop, but maybe she helps out with the clouds too. I don't know.

There is a staircase that leaves the basement and goes up to the room where I sleep. There is very little furniture in that room. A narrow bed, two chairs facing each other across a table. I don't know who brings the food but it is always on the table when I am hungry. Soup and vegetables and bread. Two carafes of water. An iron cup. I don't pay much attention to the food. I eat, drink, and spill the remaining contents of the cup out the window. Someone cleans when I am not in my bedroom. When I am not eating or sleeping, I spend most of my time in the basement. Sometimes I fall asleep there. I don't mind it. Maybe the Time Witch is in charge of the food too? I don't know. That would make sense.

I would not say that what I do makes me happy. It does not make me unhappy. Is that the same? There are days when a cloud looks very slim, when I can almost see through the fabric, when I think there is no way it can survive outside the tower. But then it floats away and I smile because I know that some of the things I do, matter.

I know we need clouds. Why do we need them? I don't know, but here I am, making them. I use a pair of scissors to cut the rolls of fabric. There is rust where the two blades meet. When I get a feeling for what shape the cloud should be, I cut that shape out and stitch it together.

Stitching takes up most of my time. It makes me anxious. I never know if I'll do it right. My breath grows short and my eyes hurt. Sometimes I hum at a high pitch or blow air through my teeth just to get rid of the jitters. I can't whistle. My tongue doesn't fold the right way. But if I could, I would. I want to shake my hands, flap my arms, jump around like a chicken until the anxiety dies off, but you can't do that when you're stitching. After a very long time, I manage to put the cloud together. I get there in the end, but that doesn't give me the confidence to believe that I'll get there next time. When the contour of the cloud is finally stitched together and it rests in my hands I feel like a minor miracle has happened. Something that has nothing to do with me, even though I made it. I hold the cloud against my chest, it soaks up my used heartbeats. I wait till it's plump and remove the brick from the wall. I feel the breeze. Sometimes rain comes in. I get a glimpse of the sky and then squeeze and push the cloud out of the tower.

I know I said I work in a basement. You are probably wondering how that is possible if I live in a tower surrounded by sky. Well, when you live in a place with no stairs to the ground, the lowest level in the tower becomes your basement. It's that simple.

When I finish with the clouds, if I have any time left, I work on the Khrónoloop. I always seem to have time for it, though. I don't know how, with all the cloud work I do. The Khrónoloop is not as important as the clouds. It is pretty, though: a blue column of light. It stretches up the wall, past the ceiling, from the basement to my bedroom. It's tall but does not take too much space. As wide as the distance from my middle finger to my elbow. I don't know why it's called the Khrónoloop. It makes no sense because it doesn't loop anywhere, it's just a straight line, but that's what I call it, I don't know why either. More of a chute if you ask me. Things are always travelling up and down: books, letters, random pieces of paper, triangles of glass or squares of plastic. Very geometrical. I just do the cleaning, and polishing, and general maintenance.

When I stick to work and sleep and take healthy walks around the basement I feel fine. Time seems to drift calmly, aside from my moments of anxious stitching, and I can live with those. But every now and again something changes. I feel empty and I can't tell why. I don't know if it has to do with the seasons or the waning of the moon, but I feel the need to remember. I stick to work and try not to think about it. Sometimes I can ignore it for what seems like a very long time. My curiosity quiets but eventually, inevitably, it comes back. I want to know more. I want to remember. This happened to me again this morning.

Let me explain: the winding staircase that leads from the basement to my bedroom does not stop there. There is a landing, and then the steps continue up to a third level. The archway that separates the landing in my bedroom from the steps that go up is barred by a heavy portcullis. In the centre of the portcullis you can see the outline of a door. It even has a handle. When I push the door it gives way. It has a lock but is never locked. Sometimes I wonder why the door is there at all. Most of the time I close it and go back to what I was doing. Not this morning.

This morning I pushed the door open and decided to walk up the stairs. I felt the emptiness inside me looking for something. I had never walked that part of the staircase. I felt more real with each step, more solid. The opposite of my clouds. The room on the third floor seemed smaller than my bedroom, even though it sits exactly on top of it. I saw a hearth with the fire already lit. Not far from it a desk and chair. There was a carving on the wall above the hearth, of an upturned vase spilling water, which made me think of my own head, empty of memories. I walked up to the desk and noticed a fountain pen with several sheets of paper by its side. I don't even know how I knew it was a fountain pen and not another type of pen, but I knew. The paper was marked at the top with the same image of the upturned vase. There was a chest on the floor, next to the desk.

I sat down. I wasn't sure what to do and for a while, I stared at the fire. I felt calm. The fountain pen seemed to slip into my hand and I wrote:

Hello,

My name is Gasparian. I don't ~~believe~~ think we've met. Or if we have I can't recall. I'm ~~am terribly~~ very sorry.

I started writing ~~to you~~ this because I don't know what else to do with the paper and pen I just found. I don't know if you exist, but ~~it gives me pleasure~~ I like to think you do.

When I finish writing this letter, I am going to fold it, over and over and over again until I turn it into a paper boat. I will take out one of the bricks on my wall and let ~~the letter~~ it sail to you. I hope you get it.

I had to stop because I didn't know what to write next. Sometimes I dream. Should I write about that? Some days they are good dreams, and some they are bad. There are always two children in my dreams: a girl and a boy. I don't know their names. We are sitting on the floor and the light from the lantern barely reaches our faces, just enough to see each other. The rice bowls are empty and our fingers are sticky after eating daifuku. We are happy. The boy turns his hands into the shape of a dog and the shadow on the shoji barks silently at us. We smile. It is windy outside and we are waiting for someone. The boy looks out the window and there's a small paper boat there, wrestling against the wind... I would rather not talk about the other dream if you don't mind. It is unpleasant and I wouldn't like to upset you without having ever met you. Besides, I don't remember it well. But I like the kindness of my first dream. I think it is good.

As I continued to think about what to write, I started to wonder about you, to think of how my letter would get to you, if it does. Will you turn one day and find a small paper boat tapping stubbornly against your window like the boy in my dream? Perhaps it must transform itself first in order to reach you. Translate from letter to boat, but the message is the same. Will it unfold and crawl into an envelope? Or get printed in a book? A magazine?

The fire cracked and I listened to it. Again, I noticed the chest on the floor next to the desk. I opened it: scrolls fell out like they were waiting to be released. The scrolls were white, tied closed with blue strips of cloth. Was I allowed to open them? I hesitated. I tapped the pen on the desk and stared at the fire.

When I unrolled the first scroll I felt disappointed. That was interesting: I couldn't remember the last time I felt disappointment...! There was something written on the scroll but it was in a language and script that I could not understand. To be honest, I can't even remember the name of the language I speak, but I knew the one on the scroll was not it. The second and third scrolls were the same. The fourth cracked. It looked much older than the others. Its characters seemed familiar but they were so faded I could not read them. The fifth roll had a series of drawings that, again, made little sense to me.

I untied the cord on the sixth scroll. The message was perfectly clear. I read it three times. I rolled it closed again, tied it with the blue strip of cloth, and placed it back in the chest.

I felt excited. I had seen that scroll before. I didn't know where but I knew I had. Was my memory coming back? A sense of belonging. The scroll was a letter, written by a man named Gasparian. It spoke about his life as a cloud maker. The Order of the Nebula. I didn't write it. To the best of my memory, the letter I had started writing to you was the first thing I had ever written. I went back to writing it:

I must live in the present.

There is so much I don't remember.

How did I get to this tower? I don't remember. If you were here maybe we could talk about it. Have you noticed how the word *could* can easily become a *cloud*? I hadn't, until now. *Could cloud*. It's almost a sentence.

I listened to the fire. I wondered whether I should go back to the basement. Soon. I had enough clouds; work could (cloud?) wait. I started rummaging through the chest again. There were more scrolls than I had realised. I found six in my language, with different dates, and two without a date. Should I date my letter? I did not know. All were letters by Gasparian.

The content was the same, even the handwriting, which was my handwriting too:

I know what I did last week, and the week before that, true, but my memory stops there. I am sorry. I wish I knew more. I feel light but empty.

When I finished reading that paragraph I didn't know what else to write. Should I keep reading? I picked up the pen without even knowing what I was doing and jotted down the first thing that came into my head.

I kept writing. I wrote everything you have just read. Everything I had seen and thought since I entered this room. I hadn't realised the morning was gone, and with it the afternoon, and now the stars were twinkling in front of the window. The window does not open, but if it did, I would leave the desk for a second, stick out my arm and pat one of those stars on the head. Will you too become Gasparian Nebula? If this isn't for you, pay no attention to what you just read. Let it drift away, change in your memory like a cloud and become something else. When I finish writing the letter I will take it with me and leave the third floor. I will go down to the basement. It will probably be cold by then. I will sit down at my workbench and fold. Fold after fold after fold. I may admire the paper boat for a while. Then I may drop it into the crackling blue stream of the Khrónoloop. Or perhaps I will take out a brick on the wall, look at the sky, and let this paper boat sail to you.

Part 2:

The Beginning of the End

Eddie W

If anyone asked him, Eddie would say he *hated* Australia. Especially in summer. It *burnt*.

Of all the places in the world his father could have sent him to he chose Queensland. North Queensland. But not North enough to be near the beach, just North enough to be annoying, in the middle of nowhere. When he Screened with his mother, practically his only contact with the outside world, Eddie complained about the clouds of green-black flies, the forty-eight-degree afternoons at Fort Julius Caesar. Neo-Pretoria was never that warm.

But as much as he liked complaining, as Eddie sat outside, on the steps of the creaky wooden porch staring at the trail of dust the horses left behind, he had to admit to himself, and only to himself, at least for now, that the last month had been ok. Even a bit magno.

Eddie's eyes went from the horses to the bullpen outside the main compound of Fort Julius Caesar, left of the road where the dust trail floated, and back. Even though the bullpen was empty, he felt that thing, the tease in his solar plexus. What was it? He scratched the back of his left arm, the scar on the triceps where the poison was imprinted on the night of the Incident. The skin had fragmented into overlapping, half-ovals that seemed about to flake but were hard as bark. It looked like a patch of scales. The doctors tried to remove it with cutaneous surgery but it wouldn't go away. Some days it was itchy as hell.

One thing Eddie liked about Fort Julius Caesar was not being himself, not being a Walerian. At least for now. It was weird, wasn't it? Usually he loved being a Walerian. People treated him differently when they found out. His friends came from wealthy, well connected Houses, but only one other kid in school came from one of the Seventeen Dynasties. Eddie was different because he came from two: the Oostanens on his mother's side, the Walerians on his father's. The Oostanens were an older family, with more cachet. They controlled protein production in the southern hemisphere. They started with genetically modified beef and then moved on to bison, buffalo, pork, and poultry. The Oostanens were one of the few Dutch families to settle in Australia hundreds of years ago. They bought ranches in the Duchy of Argentina when it was called something else, and Brazil, and then invested heavily during the resources boom. They were one of the first Houses to venture into industrial insect farming when the fears of meat shortage began, which was what eventually raised them to a Dynasty. Beef was still a product of pride, what his uncles called "their army of succulent Phoebus bulls", but no longer the money-making machine of old. The crest of the Oostanens was a plain sketch of a minotaur, front facing, the head of a bull with the body of a man. It didn't look scary or intimidating, or whatever minotaurs are meant to be; if anything, to Eddie it looked confused, distracted. Eddie's family chose the minotaur to honour their origin story, the beginning of the fortune in cattle farming. You are half bull, his mother, Lady Patricia, whispered in Eddie's ear even before those ears could make sense of what was being poured into them. Except he wasn't half bull, not really, was he? If the Oostanens were minotaurs *they* were half bull, weren't they? And he was half Oostanen and half Walerian, at *most* he could be a quarter bull. At least that's what he used to think until he saw the lighter in his father's study the day of the Incident.

If the wealth of the Oostanens was linked to pastures, land with dark soil and the animals that fed from it, the wealth of the Walerians was linked to just about everything else. The Walerians were the wealthiest Dynasty out of the Seventeen. The family crest was a Japanese hand fan. They made money out of countless things, but mostly out of money. One of Eddie's direct ancestors on his father's side created the hedge fund that began the whole thing. That led to banks, and credit, and currency exchanges, and eventually the extinction of most international currencies and the rise of the electronic Walerian Mon. How much were Eddie's parents worth? It was anyone's guess. Normals can tell you, down to the last Mon, how much money they have. They check their bank account and boom, presto, there it is, we can even count the cents! But Eddie had no idea. His parents had bank accounts, but they also had banks, which made things different. The prices of different assets fluctuated: land, stocks, art. If they auctioned their jewellery collections, how much would each item fetch? More or less than what was paid for it? Did anyone remember how much they paid for it? Did anyone care?

Eddie was a rarity. Dynasties did not mix bloodlines. It was a rule established by the Original Twenty-Six (when there were still twenty-six Dynasties, before they dwindled down to the remaining seventeen, mostly because of poor management by pampered heirs), to avoid the centralisation of power and financial resources. But Patricia Oostanen and Christian Walerian fought to be together and they managed it in the end. It was a love story. No one knew whether it was love for money and power, or each other. Maybe both? What everyone *did* know was that they had set a dangerous precedent. Patricia and Christian committed to a strict Chinese wall between their holdings and financial interests. There was great scepticism around this. Would they actually stick to it? Could they be husband and wife and industrial competitors at the same time? Because each had already assumed the Mantle of their Dynasty, and there was the promise of the Chinese wall, there was less opposition from the other Dynasties. But on one matter the Council of the Seventeen Dynasties *did* demand a guarantee. The Phnom Penh Convention was very clear on the matter of Dynastic mergers: it was illegal. What, then, would happen with Patricia and Christian's offspring? If they only had one child, would she be the Head of two separates Dynasties? Of course not. That would not avoid the centralisation of power, because you cannot build a Chinese wall within yourself. No. The Oostanen-Walerian union would have to have *at least* two children, who would inherit a Dynasty each. The arrival of Eddie's long-awaited baby sister had been postponed time and time again. It would happen, his parents assured him, everyone, the press, but at present there was much work and little time for conception. But without conception, or at least its successful aftermath, Eddie's Blood Rights would make him the most financially powerful human in history. When he made it to adulthood. If there were no further Incidents.

The horses were almost lost in the distance. The Australian grazing stations were all about beef, but in the last few years Uncle Jeremy had started breeding horses. It was one of his pet projects, like the Mefisto cattle, which were not bred for their meat, but because Uncle Jeremy liked how they looked. Differently from most of the rest of the Oostanen empire, Uncle Jeremy did not switch to genetic engineering. He was against industrial meat production. He used old breeding and rearing methods to preserve the animals' health, and the integrity of their bloodlines. The animals were fed what they should, as they should, which meant plenty of time and space for grazing. It also meant the way things were done at Fort Julius Caesar had not changed much in the last three to four hundred years. He called this "the Time Bubble", because that's exactly what living with Uncle Jeremy felt like, a different era, with bare telecoms, no weather manipulation, no privacy problems because there were no memory hacks. Uncle Jeremy squeezed orange juice in the morning with his own hands. Eddie didn't know anyone who did that anymore. It was magno.

Uncle Jeremy reared Stockhorses, a breed that could be traced to the nine original horses brought to Australia in 1788 with the arrival of the First Fleet in Botany Bay. Across Queensland and the Northern territory, Uncle Jeremy's grazing stations specialised in a crossbreed of Tajima Wagyu and Black Angus herds. The annual monsoons fed the 400,000 hectares of prime grazing country that Uncle Jeremy had looked after since he was only a few years older than Eddie, when his Blood Rights allowed him to be in control of the land. He made sure the cattle were housed comfortably, with shelter from the weather. His Mefisto bulls were a crossbreed of the Meronesa cattle from Portugal and the Fistoben of the Kirov region, which were in turn a cross of the Great Russian and Swiss Brown cattle. This mixture of Meronesa and Fistoben Uncle Jeremy affectionately portmanteaud into "Mefisto". If the Phoebuses were not great for business, the Mefistoes were much worse. The breeding was time consuming and their meat was tough, but Uncle Jeremy said their long twisting horns gave them the most majestic bearing he had seen in a bull. Was there one in the bullpen right now? The sun was on Eddie's eyes, and he couldn't quite see from here.

The screen door rattled open behind Eddie. He didn't bother to see who it was. The tread was strong but silent. Eddie felt its vibration in the wooden beams of the porch. Uncle Jeremy's walk was like a genomic signature: no two alike. He stopped by Eddie's side at the top of the porch steps. Eddie looked up at him. The set of the jaw, the dilation of the nostril, the way the muscles on the cheekbones contracted toward the nose, and that strip between the upper lip and nose, paved with the black, regrowing heads of his uncle's shaved moustache. Eddie didn't know what that part of the face was called, but it bulged right now, as his uncle looked out in the same direction Eddie had been staring at before, after the horses. Those were Oostanen-blue eyes, a very light shade of blue. Like his mother and her three brothers, until the Incident Eddie had had those blue eyes. But one of the side effects of the poison was the concentration of melanin in the stroma of his irises, which affected pigmentation, irreversibly. His mother said they were taupe now, an earthy grey, the colour of rotting leaves. She rarely said more than that about the Incident. She said it like it was a loss.

The airship is on its way, said Uncle Jeremy. We opened the North-West macroshield for it.

Eddie shrugged, then nodded. Uncle Jeremy sat next to him. He never spoke much, but that didn't matter. Uncle Jeremy was the only uncle Eddie liked. His father had no siblings, and his mother had four brothers: uncle Pieter, who looked after the Dynasty's holdings in South America and the Russo-Chinese Empire; uncle Jonas, who helped Pieter with all the industrial protein production; uncle Jörg, who was a drunk; and uncle Jeremy, who lived for his cattle. As the eldest female in the family, Eddie's mother held the Mantle of the Dynasty, and delegated responsibilities to her siblings as she saw fit (or not, like with uncle Jörg). Dynastic inheritance was matrilineal, one of the rules of the Original Twenty-Six. Only in the absence of a female scion could a male, like Eddie's father, or Eddie himself, take on the Mantle.

Eddie liked animals. He really did. That was part of what made Fort Julius Caesar ok. Eddie grew up with dogs. They were never his dogs. He wasn't entirely sure whose dogs they were, but they were everywhere. The family owned twen-ty-three apartment buildings in Neo-Pretoria, and God knew how many houses. There was the main house, of course, the Family Home, yes, in capitals, but depending on what his family was doing and what was going on in the country (or the world, for that matter), it was not unusual for Eddie to sleep in a different apartment two or three times a week, sometimes out of convenience, sometimes for safety. And there were always dogs, in every apartment, and every house. Different dogs. It was not like the same dogs travelled with the family from place to place. Each property seemed to have its own dog or dogs. At least one. Most of them friendly, some aloof. Eddie hadn't been able to figure this one out. Maybe his Mum was the one who liked dogs? She liked lavender and every bathroom, no matter where they went, always had a bunch of lavender sprigs in a vase waiting for them. Maybe it was the same with the pooches? He should really find out. The Walerians had vaca-tion homes in different parts of the world, and very, very rarely stayed in hotels. When they visited a place where they did not already have a house there was always a friend who did, and was more than happy to lend it for their stay. And again, there would be dogs to play with.

At Fort Julius Caesar Eddie had slept in the same room every night. In comparison to his normal life in Neo-Pretoria, always moving from one home to the next, at first he hated being stuck. Like a plant, no legs. Paralysed. But after the third week he started to enjoy it. The week after he arrived at the grazing station a foal was born. Eddie was there when it happened. Uncle Jeremy dragged him in to see the whole thing. It was amazing. Disgusting, and amazing. One of the farmers quietly stepped in and removed the birth sack from the foal's head to make sure it was breathing. *It*, was a he. Uncle Jeremy said he could be Eddie's horse if he wanted to look after it. There was nothing special about the horse, except that it was his. It was light brown like most of the other horses. Eddie's Mum would have called it *caramel*, the colour of one of the leather couches in his father's study. The mane was blond like a human's. Uncle Jeremy said that if Eddie wanted the horse to be his, he would have to wake up an hour early the next morning, at crack of sparrow (whatever that meant), and help him with the stump hanging from the umbilical cord, make sure it was dry, with no infections. Eddie said he would, and then went to bed and forgot all about it. He couldn't see the horse after that. Uncle Jeremy wouldn't let him. He said Eddie had been irresponsible and could not be trusted with anything as precious as a young foal. Eddie *demanded* (that was a word that often worked well for him) to see *his* horse, as Uncle Jeremy had promised he would. Uncle Jeremy locked him in his bedroom.

At Fort Julius Caesar Uncle Jeremy was all powerful. This was new. Everywhere else Eddie's parents' word was Law. Not human Law, which was discussed, negotiated, and bureaucratically legislated, which meant it could also be modified or scrapped altogether. The laws of people involved judges and police and lawyers and whatnot. The words of Patricia Oostanen and Christian Walerian were like gravity. Like time. You could throw as many tantrums as you wanted, but the Wall of the Present would never let you step into the Past. Eddie's parents were like that, better left unchallenged. And as it turned out, Uncle Jeremy was similar to them. Not the same, though, but similar. He was strict but fair. He set out the rules and did not buckle. If Eddie wanted to see the foal again he would have to earn the privilege. To Eddie's surprise, he wanted to see the foal, enough to work for it. So he did what his uncle asked for, cleaning the stables, moving buckets of shit from one place to another.

The horses had practically disappeared now. They were a moving cloud in the West, where the airship of the GC, the Global Constabulary, appeared as a black dot, flying toward the grazing station at ten thousand times the speed of a horse.

Three days after the Incident Eddie was sent to Queensland. Uncle Jeremy acted like there was nothing unusual about Eddie showing up one day to stay at Fort Julius Caesar. Macro shields were erected around the grazing stations, for security, but mostly to keep the press out. All communication with the world outside (not that Eddie was allowed that much communication to begin with), had to be through secure, monitored channels. Lady Patricia referred to the Incident as though it hadn't happened. She did not avoid the topic when it came up, she did not pretend it had not happened, but when Eddie asked a question or mentioned something in relation to the

Incident, she acted as though it were unimportant, not real, like they were talking about a fictional character who had gone through these things, not Eddie. He had not been able to speak to his father at all. He saw him once, or he thought he did, last week, by chance, as Eddie Screened with his mother. She was getting ready to go out, putting on her earrings as she stared into one of the mirrors in her bedroom and Screened with Eddie. His father appeared in the background, dressed up, lifting something from the bed. It was only for a second. Eddie asked if he could talk to him, but they were in a rush, apparently, and Eddie's mother had to go.

The airship landed by the bullpen. Uncle Jeremy patted Eddie on the arm, right on his scar. They stood up and started walking toward it. If the questions with the GC went on for long enough, maybe the horses would be back by the time they were finished. Eddie's horse was not with them. He was still a foal, not even a yearling, which apparently was what you called horses when they were a year old.

Eddie liked watching the return of the horses. It was one of his favourite things at Fort Julius Caesar. He imagined his father instead of the GC representative coming out of the airship, coming to see him. Eddie could tell him about his foal. If he stayed long enough, it would be time for the horses to come back, and they could watch them arrive together. He wouldn't admit it to anyone, but that would be magno.

The GC representative walked down the airship's ramp and headed toward Eddie and Uncle Jeremy. They met halfway between the house and the ship. She wore the red kaftan of the GC's Testimony officers, and held on to a purple briefcase on her left hand.

Uncle Jeremy nodded at the representative, but did not say anything.

Good day, Mr Oostanen. I am Constable Moffat. I believe you have a room ready for us? she said. We'll go there.

Uncle Jeremy had chosen one of the smaller bedrooms in the house for the interrogation. It was not Eddie's bedroom. There was a single bed, a wardrobe, a coffee table that had been dragged there from another room most likely, because it made no sense here, and a chair. Uncle Jeremy's house used old-fashioned light bulbs. It was still early, and there was plenty of light coming through the windows, but uncle Jeremy turned on the lights anyway. Eddie stared at the glass pear dangling from the ceiling. He liked it, however poorly and inefficiently it shone. It was hard to read the Constable's expression. Confused? Unimpressed? Offended?

Edward, as I said, I am Constable Moffat. This is going to be very easy. I am going to set up the Orb here. Just give your Testimony of the attack. I believe someone has already spoken to you about this? How it works?

Eddie nodded. His parents' legal team had instructed him on exactly what to say. He, in turn, had spoken to Cassius and Avery about it.

Constable Moffat opened her purple briefcase. She brought out the Orb, placed it on the coffee table. It was a model Eddie had not seen before. She shuffled the chair so that it stood facing the table. Please take a seat, Edward. This will not take long. Just say what happened. The facts. We could be done in fifteen minutes. It depends on you. Please sit down while I set up.

Eddie sat down.

Edward Walerian, said Constable Moffat.

The Orb levitated at eye level, and floated toward Eddie. It started taking his biometrics. Retina, sweat swab, blood, palm scan and fingerprints. The Orb was a similar shade of red to the officer's kaftan. It must be a GC model, thought Eddie. Eddie's own Orb was light blue, which had been magno a year ago. Now the cheaper models came in orange and white.

After taking Eddie's biometrics the Orb continued levitating to the ceiling, close to the lightbulb, and began its spherical recording of the room.

I am Constable Moffat. We are recording the Testimony of Edward Walerian in relation to the attempt on his life. Edward, your uncle and I are going to step out. Once we leave, please tell the Orb what happened.

The door closed behind Uncle Jeremy and Constable Moffat. Eddie stared at the Orb, then the wall. He leaned forward, the elbow of his right arm burying into his thigh, his chin cradled atop the palm of his hand like a precariously balanced capital on a column.

Three friends came to the house, said Eddie. To play. I was

sleeping at the big house that night. We keep the Levitators there because there isn't room for them anywhere else. I was with Cassius Salinas, he is Dynastic too, the only other in the School. Saul Avery, he comes from a House, but we've been friends since we were little. And Scholars. He's a Normal. He doesn't have a Mon to fall on, but he's alright. He can be very funny. So we allow him to be with us.

The Orb flashed orange. 'Scholars' is not a name, it said kindly. What is 'Scholars'' name?

Sorry, Robin Gregory. We call him Scholarship Boy because that's the only reason he's with us, *was* with us, at St Hubert's. Scholars. We were playing upstairs, the hallway with the wood panels outside Father's study. Avery and I were looking out the large window at the garden where we keep the Levitators. I was just showing him where they were. It was me on the right, then Avery, and then Cassius came too. Scholars was behind, looking at something in the hallway. I wasn't paying attention to him.

I told the guys we should go, then Scholars shoved in between Avery and me, and looked out the window. I was about to tell him to piss off for shoving in, but he made a joke and patted me on the arm, right here. Eddie pointed at the scar on the back of his upper left arm. I can't remember him touching me any other time that day, so that must have been when he imprinted the poison. I don't know how he got it into the house because security checked Scholars, Avery and Cassius when we arrived.

I wanted to go down again to play with the Levitators. We walked down the hallway, to the stairs. That's when I started feeling lightheaded. The room moved sideways and I stopped. The others kept going, and then Avery came back to see if I was ok. I fell on my face. I don't know if Scholars started sounding crazy before or after I fell. I can't remember. He said he didn't mean to. That he was sorry, or didn't want to. None of it made sense. Something about his mum being sick. Someone making her sick. Paying for the trip? He scared me. So I raised my voice and said the word to activate the house's security protocol. I think that was before I fell. I was coughing, but I passed out before the guards arrived.

Eddie sat up. He stared straight at the Orb. That's it, he

said. That's what happened. That's everything I remember about the Incident. I mean, the time when I was attacked.

He wasn't lying, strictly speaking. He just wasn't saying what happened *before* he was attacked. But that's not what they had asked him. He knew the Orb could detect lies. He waited. Because what had happened before would get him into big trouble. Maybe not today, maybe not while the furore of the Incident was still on. But if word of it got out, knowing his father, sooner or later, Eddie was going to have to pay. As he stared at the Orb, waiting, the earlier hours of the day of the Incident played back in his head. Eddie was grateful the Orb could not read his mind while he gave Testimony, just his pulse.

The four boys had had lunch and then went out to play in the garden, chasing each other in the Levitators. They did this for a while but after Cassius lost twice in a row he started saying the whole thing was boring. The Levitators had been altered as part of Eddie's security protocol. They wouldn't hover at more than a metre above ground, and their maximum speed was fifty seven kilometres per hour, which wasn't very fast. But still, it wasn't boring. Avery didn't think so, and neither did

Eddie.

They went back inside. They were a bit tired, dirty from tumbling on the grass. Sweat was starting to cool on their foreheads and the back of their necks, and their arms and legs felt light. There were milk and waffles waiting on the coffee table in one of the parlours. Two Afghan hounds, one caramel, one ash, lay next to the table, snouts between their paws. Their eyes were at an angle, looking up, fixed on the waffles, but they stayed put. Eddie had no idea what their names were. He thought the dogs were new. Cassius walked over one of the dogs and jumped on a couch. He said his Levitator went three times faster than Eddie's, and twice as high, and Avery told him to shut up, because he only had two, not five, and they were at his family's ranch because he had no room to play with them in his house, like Eddie. Scholars said nothing. He just smiled and ate his waffles.

Avery was right. Cassius needed to shut his mouth, and Eddie knew exactly what would do the trick. He bit into his waffle. Follow me, he said, mouth half-full.

Where are we going? asked Cassius.

You'll see, said Eddie.

They left the parlour and entered the ground floor kitchen. The dogs followed them until they reached the kitchen door. One of the chefs was leaning against the stove, laughing with a maid, or kitchen hand, or someone, who sat by a wooden table covered in flour. Their laughter was cut short when Eddie and his friends entered the kitchen. The chef and the maid (or, again, whatever she was) froze. Eddie ignored them. He opened a door that looked like a cupboard, slim and tall, going from floor to ceiling. It wasn't a cupboard; it was, in fact, a perfectly normal door, which led to a black, wrought iron, spiral staircase. The staircase was narrow, each step scarcely larger than the children's feet. It was perfect for them. Eddie climbed up two steps at a time. The structure shook, the black iron reverberating like a tuning fork as the three children joined him. He stopped after two floors, and opened another door. They were in a long, wood-panelled hallway with large windows that looked out to the gardens, the one he described when he gave his Testimony to the Orb. Eddie jumped twice on the thick rug that ran the length of the hallway, bringing his knees to his chest. This way, he said.

The door at the end of the corridor was wood-panelled, like the rest of the hallway, with a shiny, brass handle. Eddie knocked on it twice. Hear that? he said. It's not wood. It's covered in wood, but the door is as thick as a vault. There's steel, and iron, and other stuff in there, you'll see how heavy it is.

Cassius tried the handle, but it wouldn't move. Is it finger print sensitive? he asked.

You have your own vault? asked Scholars. In your house? That's *magno*!

Eddie smiled. Avery and Cassius laughed.

He doesn't need a vault, said Cassius. This house is a vault. Didn't you notice the half-hour security screening when we came in, Scholars? By the way, half an hour is a lot, Walerian. You should keep your team more efficient.

Eddie ignored the remark. It's genomic, he said. The lock. You need the combination too, but it won't open without the DNA of a Walerian.

Strictly speaking, that was not true. The genomic lock was meant to be calibrated not just to *any* Walerian's DNA, but *the*

Walerian's DNA, his father's. But somehow, when Eddie had tried it last, it worked. Eddie gripped the doorknob. He turned it three times to the right, then seven to the left. He held the base of the doorknob with his thumb and forefinger. The end of a needle poked out from the centre. It was almost invisible, like a wasp's stinger. Eddie knew it was there, but he realised he probably wouldn't have noticed it otherwise. The needle was black and it contrasted against the polished brass of the doorknob. But still, it was easy to miss. He gripped the doorknob tight. The sting didn't hurt. He flexed his fingers a few times before letting go, hoping there would be at least a drop of blood in the palm of his hand for the others to see. There was.

The door cracked open. There was no screech or groan. No sound whatsoever. Those titanic hinges were well oiled, the bolts smooth and functional. The room lights turned themselves on.

That's *magno*! said Scholars. Everything was magno for Scholars.

Christian Walerian's study was not huge. It was by no means small, but certainly not one of those showy spaces nouveau-riche tycoons go for. There was no golden filigree or excess marble. *The* Walerian was not obsessed with Roman Emperors. The décor was dignified, calm, almost austere. The study was rectangular, with a bay window on the opposite end of the room to where the children stood. To their left was a brick fireplace, to their right a wall covered in bookshelves. There were objects interspersed with the books, vases and figurines and God-knew what else, all behind glass, pillars of light falling on them as they would in a museum. Christian Walerian's desk was in front of the wall with the bookshelves, the bay window to his right. The heavy drapes on the bay window were slightly open, caressing the top of the caramel leather couch under them. They let the white sheer curtains show like a slip under a dress, and behind them, the gardens surrounding the Walerian estate, with pregnant grey clouds that probably presaged rain. There was a leather Ottoman under his father's desk, shaped like a cube. From where Eddie stood he could see one of its corners. It was a murder weapon. When Eddie was six or seven his father had brought him here to talk about something, Eddie couldn't remember what, because all other memories of the event were obliterated by what happened halfway through their conversation. Eddie saw a flash of dark on the floor followed by a noise, a shuffle. Something moved behind the desk and without a second thought his father kicked the Ottoman, hard enough that the desk shifted forward a good ten centimetres. There was a high-pitched plea, a desperate squeal. His father's half-stretched leg held the Ottoman against the inner side of the desk giving it short, calculated pushes. Eddie felt like he was there for an entire day, but in truth the squeal lasted a minute at most. It was a small, brown field mouse. The tail was twice the length of the body, which had been turned to mush. As Eddie whimpered at the body it reminded him of a half-eaten strawberry covered in milk chocolate. His father made him clean it up.

Scholars was right. The study *was* magno. But his expression this time had nothing to do with the size of the place. Or the décor. It was the tusks. A pair of elephant tusks that stood on each side of the modest fireplace, each almost two-and-a-half metres tall, their ends capped in bronze. Right about now, these are Father's most prized possession, thought Eddie, only because they made Cassius shut his stupid mouth.

They don't live here, said Eddie, glancing at the tusks. Father is gifting them to a friend. But he wanted to see them capped and ready before they are sent off. That's why they brought them up to the study.

Cassius smiled, sideways. He *always* smiles sideways, Eddie thought. Some people do it every now and again, but Cassius does it *all the time*. It's bloody annoying.

That's it, Walerian? asked Cassius. A pair of stupid tusks. You've seen the tusks at our house, and there's a pair in the house in the Pampas, taller than these. This is boring.

Sure, said Eddie. But these are not from genetically engineered elephants. They're real elephant tusks. We own extinction rights on the last herds, all of them. You know an engineered tusk can be as long as you want, but a real one this size, you don't see.

Definitely magno, whispered Scholars.

Cassius shrugged and turned his back to the tusks, staring at the book shelves behind Christian Walerian's desk. Scholars joined him.

They're awesome, Walerian. Don't listen to him. He's burning, said Avery.

Eddie shrugged, just as Cassius had. I don't care, he said.

Why should he care? He was a Walerian. *The* Walerian. Well, the *next* Walerian. The one to inherit the Mantle of the Dynasty when his father died. Cassius had to be impressed by the tusks. Either that, and he was too burnt to admit it, like Avery said, or he was so stupid that he didn't understand the difference between real elephants and engineered elephants. The truth was Eddie couldn't tell if it was stupidity. Even though he had tried, he could not read the expression on Cassius' face when he saw the tusks, and now he couldn't either because he had his back to him. He and Scholars kept staring at the bookshelves. The thing was, Eddie should not care about impressing Cassius, but he *did*. That was annoying.

What is this? Scholars was pointing at one of the objects behind glass, on the second shelf from the bottom.

What? said Eddie. I can't see. Oh, that's a family thing. It belonged to the first Walerian, the founder of the Dynasty.

Alastair Walerian? asked Scholars.

Of course *Alastair Walerian*, said Avery. How many d'you think there are?

It was a silver lighter, with the head of a bull engraved on it.

Do you want to see it, Scholarship? Asked Eddie.

Oh, no. It's fine, thank you.

It's ok. It's just a trinket. A toy. You can see it. You can't touch it, Father only lets Walerians touch it. But you've been good today, so you can see it. Up close even.

Eddie pressed his fingertip to the glass. The head of a needle poked out. The genomic lock opened for him. He held the lighter between his index and thumb. The truth was, Father loved that thing. It was most certainly not a trinket. It was the reason Eddie was now staring at the Orb in Uncle Jeremy's house in bloody Queensland, hoping the omission in his Testimony would not be considered perjury. It was, in fact, the only surviving belonging of Alastair Walerian's (other than his global financial empire). If his father even suspected Eddie had taken it out of the glass. Stare at the Orb, stare at the Orb…

Eddie turned the lighter between his fingers to show Scholars the back, which wasn't exciting, at all, because the only interesting thing about the boring lighter, if there was anything interesting at all, was the damn bull engraved on the front.

I *am* a bull!, thought Eddie. The idea filled him with a sudden, incomprehensible joy. The solar plexus tingled. I am a bull on both sides. The Oostansen minotaur, and with this, the lighter Alastair liked so much, the Walerians. I am not a quarter bull, I am three quarters bull, which means I am *mostly* bull… That's me, I *am* the bull. The head of a charging bull.

Alright, that's enough, Scholarship, said Eddie. Time to put it back.

Sure. Thanks, Walerian! said Scholars.

As Eddie was stretching to put the lighter back on its shelf, he faltered. The lighter slid between his fingers, and fell.

To Eddie's amazement he caught it. He did not have cat-like reflexes or anything remotely approximating them, but somehow his knees shot forward buckling his upper body like a spoon, and so did his spare hand, the right hand, which grazed a corner of the lighter, redirecting its fall between Eddie's thighs, where the thing lay nestled now, cosily.

You stupid…stupid Scholars, muttered Eddie, terrified of what did not happen. He placed the lighter back in its pillar of light and closed the glass case. You're an idiot, he said.

What? I was standing here, said Scholars. Didn't do anything.

Let's go, said Eddie. Before Scholarship breaks something.

That was close, wasn't it, Scholars? said Cassius. That would have left a few generations of your family indentured to the Walerians. From scholarship to slavery. How does that sound?

Come on. Out, said Eddie.

Cassius, Avery and Scholars left the study. Eddie closed the door behind him. The internal bolts fell into place with muted, confident thuds. They were back in the wood-panelled hallway.

And the rest, the Orb knew. They walked to the window, stared at the Levitators in the garden, and after the shock of the almost-dropped lighter Eddie felt like going out again, no matter what stupid Cassius said. Then Scholars turned out to be an assassin who imprinted poison on Eddie's left arm with a harmless pat. He had been blackmailed by a terrorist group who wanted to cause financial panic by getting rid of the Walerian successor. Truth be told, Eddie was never at risk. When the house's security system was activated there was an emergency response team by his side in thirty seconds. Still, it was bad that Scholars had gotten that far. Eddie's father said it was an error, on Eddie's part. That he should be a better judge of character by now. Not that he said that to Eddie, of course. Eddie's mother had passed on the information when they were Screening. Apparently she was of the same opinion...

The Orb turned green. There was a knock on the door and Constable Moffat stepped in, her red kaftan swishing as she approached the coffee table. All done, she said. We thank you for your Testimony, Edward, for your time and help with this matter. Everything is in order. We will be in touch if anything else is required. Pack, said Constable Moffat, addressing the Orb as she opened her purple briefcase. The Orb started its descent from the ceiling.

Eddie, said Uncle Jeremy, your father's office Screened. Can you Screen him back?

Eddie nodded. He waved goodbye to Constable Moffat and walked to his room closing the door behind him. Out the window he could see the bullpen, the Constable's airship in front of it like a giant, metallic grasshopper. Eddie sat in front of the dressing table in his room and stared at the mirror. It was an antique piece of furniture, late twentieth century or thereabouts, but it had been updated to be able to Screen through the mirror. Eddie took off his left shoe and started massaging the sole of his foot to calm himself. Father had Screened? he thought. Is that what Uncle Jeremy said? It has to be about the Testimony. But is he happy or angry about it? Eddie pressed harder into the pressure points on his foot, but he felt no more calm.

Father, he said.

The mirror turned white. Tammi Lou, one of Eddie's father's assistants, the one in charge of family matters, was on the line. She smiled.

Hello, Eddie.

Hello, Tammi. Father wants to talk to me?

Oh, no. He just stepped into a meeting, unfortunately. But he asked me to let you know that your Testimony was excellent. You do not look weak. At all. If anything, you look bored.

We can spin that. It's going to be good for us. You are resilient. Not even a direct attack can get to you. The future of the Dynasty is already in good hands. You not only survive, Eddie, you thrive, and you have better things to think about than a silly, hopeless attempt on your life. Anyway, bottom line, don't talk to anyone about this, ok. It's a Code Red. By next week the anticipation will be apex and we'll do something for the press. Your friends Cassius and Saul still need to give their Testimonies, and we just need to make sure everything matches. Until then, keep up the good work. I'll tell your Father you said hi.

Tammi waved and the Screen went white again. Eddie saw himself in the mirror.

He looked out the window. The Constable's airship lowered its ramp for her to go in. She was standing at the foot of the ramp, talking with Uncle Jeremy. Well, she seemed to be doing most of the talking while Uncle Jeremy nodded. Still, that was unusual. What on Earth were they talking about? You know what else is unusual? thought Eddie. Cassius and Avery not giving their Testimony yet. Why did Eddie have to go first, when he was hidden here in the middle of nowhere? Maybe, because you're the one who was attacked? said a voice in his head. Fair point. Hopefully Avery and Cassius would stick to the deal and not say anything about the lighter episode in the study. They wouldn't be asked about it directly so there is no reason they should. Avery was solid, he wouldn't betray Eddie. Cassius' silence had cost Eddie a pretty penny: two Levitators and a gyro-Orb. Well worth it if he kept his word.

Uncle Jeremy and Constable Moffat were still talking. Something in the distance, behind them, caught Eddie's eye. The blotched speck of black seemed to have a long, long hand (even though it was an animal, and therefore, handless), long enough to cross the bullpen and reach inside Eddie's stomach and squeeze hard, like Uncle Jeremy did with those oranges that became juice in the morning. There it was again, that tease of the solar plexus.

It was a bull. Of course it was a bull. What else would be in the bullpen at this time of the day? Eddie hadn't seen it before though, when he was waiting for the airship. Had he? A glorious black bull, wide as a rhino-tank, with magnificent horns. Eddie couldn't see the colour of the horns from this distance, it was too far (which only spoke to the animal's size), but he imagined them off-white, with a tinge of yellow, like nicotine-stained fingers. A shiver went up Eddie's spine, and his head tingled. He scratched it.

The bull moved fast. Very fast. It was charging from the opposite side of the pen. Lost in their conversation, Uncle Jeremy and Constable Moffat seemed completely unaware of it. Then the bull slowed down as it approached the bullpen barrier and veered to the right, following the circle of the enclosure. Now that the charging was over it seemed to have stepped into a cheerful trot, a bull's equivalent of a mosey. Constable Moffat turned and entered her airship. The ramp was raised and closed. The airship took off and disappeared in the direction it came from.

What had happened? Why did the bull do that? Did Uncle Jeremy and Constable Moffat take any notice? They didn't seem to. Was it the Constable's red kaftan that excited the bull? Was that actually a thing? Bulls went for red? And why did it stop and turn around? Eddie was perplexed, and fascinated. Uncle Jeremy stood staring at the sky, as if he could still see the airship that was far gone. There was no indication the horses were on their way back.

Eddie's mind started working. It took away the worry of Cassius' and Avery's Testimonies, the aftertaste of the Incident, and pushed them somewhere they could not hurt him. Instead, something hot and tingly started running up and down his arms, travelling back to his stomach, then the legs, where he could feel it in the back of the knees, sticky and warm. It tugged back his shoulders, pushed forward the chest. The sensation came with a very clear image, something his imagination was furiously putting together, bit by bit, block by block. An idea. A hypothesis. It was impossible, but it felt free. Good.

What if the charging bull had not stopped? Was one of Uncle Jeremy's Mefistos strong enough to bring down the wooden fence? What if it had climbed up the airship's ramp, all the way to Constable Moffat in her red kaftan and…? Even better: what if the victim on the ramp was not Moffat, but Christian Walerian, visiting Eddie to ask him how he was and talk about his new foal. The images brewing in his brain were nonsense, paved with one *what if* after another. But what if? Is that where his feeling of freedom came from? Eddie imagined the animal's majestic haunches, the nostrils steaming with rightful anger. And then the trampling hooves, the horns swooping down and up again, and up and down in powerful arches, the silhouettes of wings that could bear Eddie to freedom.

Ganeshiya

A grey note filled the air, a cement note the colour of an Elephant's haunch.

The rituals of Elephants came before the world. But this Song of Change was not the Elephants'. It had seldom been used. In fact, it belonged to the Time Witch, Edith of Endor, Translator and Necromancer.

The unison chant broke into counterpoint. The notes anchored themselves in the sutures of reality and began to pull. Ganeshiya's assassination had created an untimely vacuum. Life was out of balance. But together Amerintha (ancient of the Ancient Elephants, Empress of her Race) and the Time Witch, could make it right. Had she still been in the habit of using language in the old way, the Time Witch would have called this 'a Translation of Essence', because it wasn't quite a transmigration, in the traditional sense of the word. It was the process that helped the indispensable quality of Ganeshiya, the Elephant, to have a different form, much like meaning when it travels from one language to another. But the Time Witch had transcended Time, and with it, her old approach to linear, sequential language, and so she stood in rude silence, bored and a little fidgety.

The Elephant Elders remained motionless, the Ancients stomped their feet. Edith of Endor brought the Khróno Lance out of her robe, which was deep as the night sky and carried as many secrets. A round, golden medallion dangled from her neck. She unscrewed the Lance at the middle, separating it into two wands: Future and Past. One she held to the clouds, the other she buried in dark soil. No one knew which wand was which. She yawned. The bluish-white light of the Khrónoloop jumped between the two wands.

Ganeshiya's features changed. The empty, bleeding holes where his tusks had been, healed. The creases on his forehead, a badge of wisdom and rank in Elephants–like growth rings on trees–were almost gone too; only four, imperceptible, puny little lines remained. The skeleton adapted from quadruped to biped, effecting the changes needed for the upright spine and weightless arms, which could not compare to his former tree-felling columns of muscle and bone. Elephant eyes see what human eyes cannot. The saddest thing about this change, this unusual 'Translation', reflected Amerintha, was to see Ganeshiya's memory go. Like the useless, pre-infantile appendage that now puckered out from the centre of Ganeshiya's face where his proud proboscis had been, his memory was reduced to the size of a pea. Amerintha saw it evaporate until only crucial fragments (his name, his mission, his family, the most basic history) could fit into the tiny hypothalamus. It was gone. If he was lucky he would remember a few hundred years, at most. But the memories of their bloodlines, passed from the First Elephant to the calf who had just dropped from the womb… those were gone. Another lost gem amongst the ever-diminishing trove of Amerintha's people.

Ganeshiya lay on the dry grass. He remembered why he

was here. He remembered how to stand up and walk like an Elephant. He also remembered seeing humans walk. Soon enough he would figure out how to walk like a human. But the rest, this... this *forgetting* he did not understand. A crumbling, shifting memory of one hundred and fifty-seven years left little room for introspection. They remember lies and make up truths, these humans, he thought, which explains a lot about them.

As we said before, in order to transcend Time, Edith of Endor had had to transcend language a long time ago, or re-invent it, so it was no surprise to anyone that she left without saying a word. The circle of Elephants began to disperse. Untha, Amerintha's great grand niece, turned from the solemnity of Ganeshiya's transformation to the solemnity of new grass and began to feed. Her son, Jelelem released a long, powerful stream of urine with equal devotion to the present. The pachyderms moved away from Ganeshiya, except Amerintha. Eventually, Ganeshiya was able to stand up. With a swing of her trunk delivered midriff Amerintha landed him back on the ground. He stood up and tried to return the affectionate welcome by punching the Empress on the forehead. He lost his balance and fell.

You know what you have to do, Amerintha said. *It is time we end this.* She told him again the story of Circular Time, in case this new, little brain of his had already forgotten it, the war against the forces of the Charging Bull, and the need to recruit an army.

Amerintha gave him clothes. She dressed him in a white linen shirt, shorts and sandals. He wished he could bellow at her, show his love and gratitude before leaving, but he knew how futile such longing was, because Amerintha, Goddess of all the Herds that had ever been and would ever be, knew him inside out.

You have nothing to thank me for. I send you to Battle. I send you to Pain and Doubt. It will not be easy.

He walked away. From a distance his family trumpeted their goodbyes, but eventually they returned to the business of the Present. Ganeshiya was leaving and that was that.

*****

He travelled for a very long time. His orientation was not as good as he thought it would be with this new hypothalamus. Never before had he felt so exposed. With his generational memories and his connection to the Herd obliterated, he was a little nothing adrift in the world. Who was this 'I' that kept popping up in his thoughts with no relation to the higher 'We'? It was hard to understand. The memory of his communal Elephant identity lingered, but it overlapped with an arrow in his awareness, this new way of being, the 'me, me, me'.

Ganeshiya found a tree behind a farmhouse and sat under it. A cat joined him. Despite Ganeshiya's new shape the cat identified him as an Elephant and paid its respects, purring and rubbing its back against the side of his stretched legs. A grey cat with brown spots on its fur. Ganeshiya had not come across any humans since he had left the Herd. Aside from the jeep tracks leading away from his murder site, this new vista—ploughed lands, fences, the farmhouse, and now the domesticated cat—was the first sign of human habitation he had seen in seven days.

He and the cat lost track of time, playing. When the young woman came out of the farmhouse with a bowl of milk calling its name, the cat perked its ears but stayed put by Ganeshiya's side. Then she saw Ganeshiya and gasped, dropping the bowl. The milk splashed. How strange, thought Ganeshiya. She scuttled back into the house and Ganeshiya went back to playing with the cat.

Again, the young woman came out of the house, this time accompanied by someone. Ganeshiya raised his head to look at them; the cat didn't bother. The young woman was pointing at him. Her companion was a wrinkled, bent old lady. The old lady squinted her eyes, her mouth fell open. She grabbed the young woman's hand, stepped over the smashed bowl of milk, and they started walking toward him.

The cat was on its back playing with a loose thread that hung from the left cuff of Ganeshiya's shirt. He saw the two women approaching. When they were two metres away from Ganeshiya the old woman fell to her knees and pulled the young one down with her. The former shook her head, vigorously.

Shri! Shri! Vighneshvara! Ganpati! It is you, you have come!

Yes, it was him, and he had come. He said as much. The old woman pressed her forehead to the floor and wept. Come, said Ganeshiya, we've got work to do.

The old woman's name was Fatima. She and her daughter became Ganeshiya's first acolytes. They left Fatima's daughter's husband's farm that very instant, and started roaming the Earth with the Elephant Man.

*****

Ganeshiya would never think of calling the thing on his face a trunk. It was clearly a nose. A very long nose, a bulbous nose, but at the end of the day, a mere nose. There was nothing trunk-like about it. It didn't have the girth, length, strength, or majesty of even the flimsiest trunk. Others didn't seem to think the same.

To his surprise, they encountered very little resistance. A day after they left the farm, Shuba's husband, for Shuba was the young woman's name, caught up with them in his truck.

Fatima and Shuba were tired, their saris starting to tear around their feet. Covered in dust as they were, they looked like two raw, crumbed tropical fish about to be thrown into the fryer. When the truck stopped, the grey cat nestled by Ganeshiya's feet. It could tell this was going to be good.

Shuba's husband stepped out. He didn't bother closing the door. He ordered his wife and mother-in-law to get in. Both said no. He repeated the order, and the women repeated their refusal. He said he had ordered them nicely the first two times, and now things were going to get messy. He bent inside the truck and picked up his shotgun. He aimed it at the root of the Elephant Man's nose.

Ganeshiya stomped his foot. The ground shook and Shuba's husband fell, dropping his weapon. The shotgun fired. Neither Fatima nor Shuba screamed, but the man did. He scrambled back to his feet as fast as he could. He picked up the shotgun. The barrel was stuffed with flowers.

Shuba's husband screamed again, and he dropped the shotgun again, and again, it fired. More flowers.

You may join us if you want, said Ganeshiya.

Shuba's husband did, and from that day on, decided not to speak another word.

*****

Ganeshiya refused to fly or take a boat. His Herd walked. Walking brought them together. It gave them time to think. The changing landscape gifted them with peace. They weren't flying anywhere.

They gathered behind Ganeshiya by the thousands. At nightfall, Ganeshiya stomped his feet and the trees gave fruit. When it started to rain some complained but Ganeshiya told them to take off their clothes and learn to live like Amerintha, like the Ancients, the First Elephants. Someone asked who the First Elephants were. What on Earth was he talking about? Do tell us, Ganpati. Tell the story so we can understand it! Go on, Shri Shri, do!

Ganeshiya was sitting under a tall tree with long branches and heart-shaped leaves. The grey cat jumped from the ground to his shoulder, where it draped itself around Ganeshiya's neck, purring.

Stories are infinite, said Ganeshiya. They contain everything and nothing, depending on who listens, and where, and when. They are, like every symbol in the history of the Universes, the vessels of meaning. He paused, unsure what to say next. That sounded a bit grandiose, but useless. A fly landed on his nose but he didn't want to swat it away. They wanted the story of Circular Time, and the war to come, the story that Amerintha had repeated to him before he left. It lay dormant in their blood, hibernating in their genes. Was this spring, metaphorically speaking? Was this the right time to awaken the narrative?

As good as any, thought Ganeshiya. Why else am I here?

Ganeshiya was determined and confident, but inexperienced at telling tales. Storytelling was not something practised by Elephants, amongst whom there was no need for repetition.

The River of Time flows neither forward nor backward, said Ganeshiya. Because Time is not a River, it is a Loop. Again, empty verbosity. Oh, damn it all. Here we go, and let it be whatever it will, he thought.

It starts with an army of bulls, in Australia, Ganeshiya cleared his throat. Or maybe it began in Alexandria, or that scrawny village North of Holland they called Oostzaan, East of the river Zaan? In Neo-Pretoria? Maybe it was that bloody Silvius. I don't know. See? This is the problem with the story of Circular Time, that beginnings and endings become redundant and confusing. But we must start somewhere, so what the hell, let's start with the man in the clouds.

CloudMan lived in a tower in the sky. He was put there by his own sister, the Time Hag, who kidnapped him when he was still a child. His memory was wiped. CloudMan was led to believe that his job, his only purpose in life, was to make clouds, following in the footsteps of a Holy Order devoted to that very purpose, the Gasparian Nebulas. A saddlebag of poppycock if you ask me, but the story was effective. It kept CloudMan busy and not terribly worried about his real job, which was giving maintenance to the Khrónoloop, the true axis of our story.

The Time Witch thought that kidnapping CloudMan was a kindness, that it would protect him from the war to come. This is debatable, and not for me to judge. All families have compli-cated stories. The point here is that a bloody, messy war was, in-deed, coming. Or it is coming, because we haven't reached that part of the tale yet. Damn circularity to a circle of Hell where not even Silvius will be able to find it, but again, what I just said will make no sense to you until later. Anyway, the Time Hag created the Khrónoloop to recruit her army, the Opposition, a force powerful enough to resist the rise of Hypermercantilism and the sadism of Walerian's minotaurs. That's where the con-federacy of bulls comes in. I don't know if you'll be told this part of the story later on, so let's have it now.

The army of bulls were descendants of a wretched ab-erration, a primitive genetical experiment that bore unhealthy results. Phoebus, the demented bull. One of our agents tried to stop him, but alas, poor Laurel's failures are irrelevant here. The army of bulls began, somewhat innocently as part of the Oostanen cattle business. The meat of these beasts was mouthwatering. As a side effect, they were formidably aggres-sive. Somehow, however, inexplicably, they followed orders from certain farmhands. A paradox. It turned out the bulls' bellicose instincts could be harnessed, not just figuratively. A few more years of genetic and behavioural experiments, collate research across fifteen state-of-the-art laboratories, endless funds, and Walerian eventually got his man-cow hybrids to bend the other Dynasties to his will when they opposed his rise to power after his sister's death. Or murder. No one's sure. We have no smoking neutrino blade.

The Witch travelled the Circle of Time, enlisting those who could help her. I am one of them. *We* are part of that army. Spoiler: we lose. The Hypermarket will rise, but that is not the point. There is no final battle once time becomes a loop. The important thing is balance, the counteracting force, the Opposition. This is what we are here for. Was that clear? Did it make sense? I am happy to take questions now.

A forest of hands went up, everyone wanted to interrogate him. But that was fine. He knew there would be questions. After the first telling, confusing as it may have been, Ganeshiya felt better. By the time he finished answering questions and re-telling the story, the sun had been up for a while and birds had stopped chirping at the dewdrops. Everyone who was assembled at the foot of the mount was cold, exhausted and rheumy eyed, but not one person had fallen asleep. The smell of insomniac halitosis filled the air as one thousand and one jaws dropped in amazement. So that was the story of Circular Time. And incredible and convoluted as it sounded, it made sense when you heard it from Vighneshvara's lips. Even if it took him a few times.

Ganeshiya stood. On the floor, the grey cat stretched and trembled like a plucked harp string. It was time to go.

*****

Ganeshiya followed Miss Grace Hiu from one sumptuous room to the next. The grey cat was his only companion.

Miss Hiu had expressed some interest in Ganeshiya's cause. She was the daughter of Ma Hiu, head and principal heir of one of the seventeen Mercantile Dynasties, the House of Hiu. She had invited Ganeshiya to her town house for tea or a drink with one condition: he must come alone. His thousands of followers must stay outside the city. The cat had been a last-minute concession.

So far, Ganeshiya had refused to meet with politicians, gangsters, and billionaires, who were, for the most part, remarkably similar. When Miss Hiu's envoy arrived with an Orb on a silver tray, it started ringing and, to his surprise Ganeshiya answered. Not only did he answer, but he also agreed to Miss Hiu's invitation. His acceptance came out instinctively. It left his lips without him being able to stop it, like a belch. It made Ganeshiya suspect there were larger forces at play here.

Miss Hiu was starting to feel slightly irritated. The Elephant Man seemed completely unimpressed by anything she said. She was used to engaging with her guests in a language of polite agreement: she showed them something – a Rembrandt, a Fabergé egg – and they politely agreed with her on how lovely it was. She would talk about travel and food and her homes around the world, the clothes she was wearing, and she would politely give them advice on how to emulate her, which her guests were always thankful. But the Elephant Man was unresponsive. He walked through the great rooms of her mansion as though he were roaming the jungle, scarcely noticing the treasures her father had hoarded for her.

They sat down to tea in one of the house's many parlours. Miss Hiu did not sigh, but she certainly felt like it. After tea, the Elephant Man would be shown out, and she could go back to her life without this feeling of…unease. She noticed he was staring at one of the glass cabinets by the window, a tall, restored piece of furniture. Oh, good, she thought, we're back on familiar territory. That silver tureen, the entire set as a matter of fact, belonged to Frances Nelson, the admiral's wife, she said. There is a lovely 'N' inscribed in the centre, festooned with garlands. But enough talk from me, Ganpati! You have scarcely said a word! Now *you* tell me something, do. I have been dying to hear about your protest. Can we call it a protest? See, I am so curious! It is the very reason I wanted you to come here, to talk about it, not to show you my silly trinkets. What are you after? Why assemble these people in peaceful walks around the world without revealing your purpose? If you tell me and I am convinced, I may be able to help you. Please, take a seat. Refreshments should be here shortly.

The housekeeper pushed a trolley into the parlour. A five-tiered, silver cake stand stood in the middle, brimming with scones, sandwiches and fresh slices of apple and melon. Behind the housekeeper came another maid who started unloading the teapot, cups and saucers, spoons, crémière, lemon, and milk. The two women populated the coffee table between Ganeshiya and Miss Hiu with the implements of tea. They moved quietly, in particular the housekeeper. Miss Hiu ignored them. You have barely spoken, Miss Hiu said. Are you hungry, Ganpati? Please, help yourself. Maybe a scone? Will you tell me more after a scone?

The cat jumped on Ganeshiya's lap. The Elephant Man scratched its chin. Miss Hiu kept talking but he was not listening. His eyes had reached the mirror above the mantelpiece before him. They froze there. He could sense the Khrónoloop behind the fireplace, its bluish-white aura buzzing like a power line in the rain, but that was not what caught his attention. What hijacked his gaze stood in front of the mirror: his tusks, those half-moons of ivory belonged to the temporal, not the immortal race of Elephants. He had changed, translated, he had transcended them, transcended flesh in the same way he needed to transcend this moment of horror. What hidden truth lay in this place? What catapult to wisdom? If Amerintha were here, what would she do? He felt the tear ballooning at the corner of his right eye. It grew like a round pearl but did not burst. A pea, a golf ball, a watermelon…splash! That's the way a semi-god cries, tears like small planets. And now the left eye…Miss Hiu screeched, What's wrong, Ganpati! Ganpati, why do you weep so? Talk to me!

She stood and screamed at the housekeeper and the maid, who were waiting by the cake trolley. We need towels, bring towels!

Ganeshiya started sobbing. Miss Hiu grew frantic. She took off her raw-silk jacket to try to contain the new tear, but the moment the two came in touch the tear burst. Splash! A bucketful of water on the floor, droplets on her ankles. Why on Earth was the housekeeper taking so long? thought Miss Hiu.

Miss Hiu walked to the other side of the room. She was revolted, but also slightly moved. She opened the glass cabinet and brought out Fanny Nelson's tureen. The third tear was rapidly forming out of Ganeshiya's right eye. Miss Hiu brought the rim of the silver tureen to it. The tear slid down, gracefully, rolled past the centre of the tureen to the opposite end and back, like a teenager in a skate park. Once at the centre, it lost its shape and dissolved into a shallow puddle. Miss Hiu knelt in front of the Elephant Man. When the fourth tear came out of the left eye, Miss Hiu repeated the process, collecting it in the tureen. By then the housekeeper had returned with an armful of towels, but Miss Hiu dismissed her. She continued collecting the Elephant Man's tears until he started calming down, his sobs eased into soft, long breaths, and he fell asleep. Between her arms, Miss Hiu held a full tureen of Ganeshiya's tears.

The cat jumped back on Ganeshiya's lap. The Elephant Man began to snore. The sound was dark, long and deep, a window to the stars. Miss Hiu found it relaxing. Her back was starting to hurt from leaning forward with the tureen, so she shook a cushion from the armchair behind her, and knelt down on it. She dipped a finger in the tureen and put it in her mouth. To her surprise, it was sweet.

The air glimmered around the contours of Ganpati's shape, or it may have been a trick of the light. By this point, Miss Hiu was tired and uncertain. But she knew that the sleeping figure of the Elephant Man was beautiful beyond words. Without knowing why, she took off his sandals and placed his feet in the silver tureen, which splashed messily. As best she knew how to, she started washing them.

*****

The image of his tusks reflected in Miss Hiu's mirror was something Ganeshiya would never forget. Was it now part of the collective memory of all Elephants? He did not know. Irrespectively, it was an unnatural sight. An Elephant is not meant to encounter his own tusks as separate entities to his body. Miss Hiu said someone had gifted them to her father, a dignitary or business partner or someone along those lines, and her father had in turn given them to her. Was it François Ambani? Christian Walerian? Giovanni Mittal? Wasn't Walerian the hunter? she really couldn't remember.

The tusks had brass-plated bands and stood on a matching brass mount on top of two wooden bases. Ganeshiya had his back to them when he entered the parlour in Miss Hiu's house. Miss Hiu's decorator had made sure the tusks were carefully positioned so that visitors sitting precisely where the Elephant Man sat could have an almost perfect, symmetrical view of the prized trophies' reflection in the mirror above the mantelpiece.

Ganeshiya's tears were more than tears to Miss Hiu. The act of cleaning the semi-God's feet was one of the most rewarding experiences of her life. She felt cleansed after. Nothing, not one of the countless treasures cluttering her many houses had ever made her this happy.

Miss Hiu joined the inner sanctum of Ganeshiya's followers, which now comprised Fatima the Old; Shuba the Young; Shuba's husband, the Mute who, like Lot's wife, shall remain unnamed; and the Wise Grey Cat. They continued their march across the world, stomping their feet through deserts and jungles and cities and tundra, gathering more and more acolytes for the army. To those external to the movement who had not heard the story of Circular Time, the Elephant Man's peaceful global protest, if it could be called that, did not seem very clear in what it protested against, or what it supported, for that matter. Like a Herd, they were moving from one place to another, never flying, always walking walking walking walking...

The truth was, Ganeshiya was unsure of how to spread the story of Circular Time beyond his current followers, even though they numbered hundreds of thousands. How big was the army meant to be? He did not know. Amerintha had not said, and he could not find a figure in his diminished memory. He did not think himself a prophet, or even a good storyteller, but it seemed everyone wanted him to be both. He was confused. He had questions. How to make them understand that sacrifice was salvation? Not sacrifice in the morbid, gory way most humans understood it, but as it played out in the story of Circular Time. The sacrifice of fraternity. There were times when the need of the individual must be put on hold for the good of the Herd. When and how? were the magic questions. When did one step over the line to the detriment of Self, and thus, the detriment of the Herd? But when was this a good thing? A part of him understood it, but there was little logic to it, in the conventional sense that humans adhered to. Language failed him when he tried to explain these ideas to himself. The

Time Hag would have known what to say, or what *not* to say.

Some days he had more doubts than others.

Ganpati, shall we sleep here tonight? Or would you like us to keep walking until the Evening Star goes to sleep in the morning? asked Shuba, the Young. Did it matter? the semi-God wondered. By the time his decision reached the very last follower, after the hundreds of thousands knew it, night would be gone anyway.

The Wise Grey Cat had slothfully collapsed by Ganeshiya's feet. It stretched sideways, then started licking, alternating between its back paws and genitals. Ganeshiya trumpeted a sigh. We stop, he said.

Shuba's husband, the Mute, turned to face the crowd. He raised a hand, palm stretched outward like a traffic officer, and the marchers stopped. Had there been a helicopter filming the scene, the cameras would have caught the ripple moving through the crowd, the wave of command that travelled across the files halted everyone. Until a few weeks ago there *had* been cameras and journalists swarming Ganeshiya's gigantic retinue, but before long they too joined the march, as did the journalists sent to replace them, and the replacements' replacements. The same went for the paratroopers and two different national armies; even Miss Hiu's father, the great Ma Hiu, was now treading the globe, the governance of his Dynasty passed on to the next scion.

Ganeshiya stomped his feet and the evening's meal materialised for the crowd. Fruit and fish, wine and water. From a pyramid of peaches, he grabbed the topmost and started walking in the direction of the forest.

Vighneshvara, will you not eat with us? asked Miss Hiu.

Not tonight, he said.

He walked until the murmur of the crowd was drowned by the murmur of the forest. Where his bare feet trod, clumps of red flowers grew, no bigger than a button. This was new but Ganeshiya did not notice the wake of ripening buds he left behind, like ship tracks after parting waters. The Wise Grey Cat did, however, and it scrunched its nose at the sickening pollen. In his left hand, Ganeshiya held the ripe peach, with his right he stroked his cheeks, clasping them softly between thumb and fingers, then sliding both down the length of his jaw to his chin. As an Elephant, he had never been able to touch his tusks, except with his trunk. They were a pair of parallel needles pointing in the right direction, which was wherever he wanted to go. That grounding majesty, the certainty of purpose they gave him was gone.

He reached a clearing in the forest. It was as steeped in darkness as the walk to it had been, but at least now he could see the stars. He sat down with his back to a tree. A massive tree, he realised, a Montezuma Cypress. A moment of recognition: Laurel, is that you, dear friend? he asked. The bark responded by cuddling his back, almost, but not quite, with the tenderness of an Elephant's hide. The Wise Grey Cat's paws padded the grass around Ganeshiya, and then the soft patch of darker darkness jumped on Ganeshiya's lap. The Elephant Man stroked the cat's back and stared at the stars as he rested with his back against Laurel. What do you want me to do now, Amerintha? he asked aloud.

The first part of his mission, to tell the story of Circular Time, seemed accomplished. Somewhat. He hoped. What now? How were they to prepare for battle?

Oh, how he missed his tusks! Had Amerintha made the right choice when she revived him after the treacherous hunters were done with him, Christian Walerian and his friends? Ganeshiya felt she hadn't. He did not feel like the great Ganpati everyone claimed he was. When his followers cried *Vighneshvara! Vighneshvara!* with arms outstretched and that look of devotion on their faces, his stomach turned.

The Wise Grey Cat snuggled against his neck, pushed his chin up. Laurel whispered an ancient song from her trunk in the language of flowers. The constellations hadn't always been the same, but Ganeshiya couldn't remember what they were like before. The Chameleon, the Water Snake, the Peacock, the Keel and the Chisel, the Herdsman, the Charioteer and Water Bearer he could spot without trouble. He remembered being able to remember the old formations when he was an Elephant, his effortless ability to summon them. *That* he could recall, but the secret of their names, the patterns of the ancient stars his people gazed upon hundreds of thousands of years ago, were gone.

The Khrónoloop

Edith stared at the wall behind her desk. The granules of grout had at some point been white. Now they were grey. Dusty and disgusting. A copy of the only photograph she had of her brother Peter was stuck to that wall with a good blob of Blue Tack. She used to have the photograph as a screensaver on her Orb. But since we were told Orbs were more addictive than cocaine and had severe effects on the mesolimbic pathways of the brain leading to memory loss, attention deficit, and loss of libido, we had to give them up, print our pics, and go back to Blue Tack, she thought. In that photograph, Peter's face looks the same as Edith's. They are not *the same*, they are fraternal twins after all, but she can see the blueprint of their zygotic connection behind the mask of gender: an unusually angular face, like it's been assembled with triangles; black hair; pointy ears to balance the pointy chin. Their mother's eyes turned slightly Caucasian by the pinch of salt Dad added to the genetic soup. In that photo both still had perfect foreheads; the triangular scar above Edith's left eyebrow came after. The photograph was taken two months before the Russo-Chinese occupation of Fukoaka, which led to the annexation of Kyushu. By the time of the occupation, Edith's family was out of Japan and resettled in Neo-Pretoria. And then, when everything seemed to be finally fine and safe, Peter disappeared. A paper boat in the night, tapping on their window…but Edith did not like going there. She preferred to stay in this photo: a warm, windy evening sitting on the tatamis after dinner. Peter is teaching her how to make a shadow dog with her hands. He can't whistle, so she does it for him. There's a knock and their mother slides the screen door open and walks in with a plate of sweet daifuku…

Peter's memory was a bittersweet break. But when Edith stopped looking at the photograph her mind went back to

Hell. Well, not Hell itself, clearly, but to the Khróno-text she had finished translating, which was about Hell. In the text, the main character travels to Hell to see his mother for the last time. Bad Dante. Written in Neng (New English), which was not easy to translate, but not as bad as other periods in the linguistic future. *Clearly*, the text was an allegory. There was no question about that. But Edith had not been able to figure out *what* it was an allegory for. She had written as much in her report, and sent it off to Walerian after sending the transcription of the original to Archives and Records. Well, not Walerian himself, because the Deputy Head of the Department would never stoop to reading his own messages, but to Walerian's assistant.

And it is frustrating! And annoying, and embarrassing, she thought. Interpreting a future text was her bread and butter, so being stuck with something as important as the meaning of an allegory felt like a failure. It doesn't feel like a failure. It *is* a failure. What else would it be? she asked herself.

Edith tried not to think about it. Not because she didn't want to, but because she was exhausted. Her attention had latched on to the problem and it wouldn't let go, even after sending her report. The only way to figure this out was rest. Rest, and time, and maybe bouncing her ideas off someone else. Damn. She flicked a paper clip off her desk and it hit the wall.

She stepped out of her office and locked the door, which she hadn't done in a while. Both bolts. You never knew, with everything that was going on in the Department, and it was better to be safe than sorry. She read the metal plaque, all three lines of it, hammered onto the door:

Dr Edith Crossman

Head of Khróno-Translation

Specialisation: Future into Present

Easy to be the Head of a Centre when it's a Centre of one, she thought. Edith rushed down the stairs. Maybe she didn't *rush*, it was definitely a brisk descent, but elegant and composed, á la Edith. There was nothing relaxed about it, though. Her muscles were tired from the stress. If she didn't get some blood flowing, movement, change, a new perspective…

Edith reached the second mezzanine and observed her colleagues moseying up and down the corridors in the relaxed manner of bureaucrats who know they have work to do and not enough time to do it, but have given up on others' expectations of efficiency.

Down another flight of stairs, to the second floor. She was thirsty. I should probably go to the canteen and buy something before they close, she thought. That can be my break. She turned left, looked at the office floor on level one over the staircase's railing. Something was wrong. Here, the calm she had just seen in the Mezzanine upstairs above level two was being sucked away by something. There was a crack in the everyday workings of the office. Edith noticed it in the mannerisms that took over the floor. Tense necks, shoulders pulled back prepared for battle or a speedy flight. Artificial silence. A minor crisis? Oh…Edith could see it now. Not a crisis. A threat, a potential threat, rather, and one everyone on the floor would be wise to avoid.

The Deputy Head of the Department of Khrónographic

Affairs, Edward Ecgberht Walerian, Third Earl of Hunting-tower, had come down from his office to the first floor. Gazes snapped down. A coat of flustered, productive busyness was brushed on every paper shuffle and pen stroke. Walerian was not an imposing figure. He did not command respect from his subordinates. He was a petty tyrant. A spoiled twenty-five year-old-boy in the costume of a man, with just enough intelligence to understand pain and how to best inflict it on others. A bureaucratic sadist. He was also the inheriting scion of one of the Seventeen Dynasties. The Walerians had a monopoly on banking. And data trade, and sport, and pornography, and renewable energy, and arms manufacturing. They owned half of the former USOA, the Post-Patagonia stretch, most of Neo-Pretoria, and only God knows what else. Everyone at the Department had a job; they worked. But this wasn't work for Walerian. It was a box he had to tick. And it was also a game because there were no consequences to it. His future positions had been mapped by his parents, decided and secured. He was being groomed for power, to inherit the Mantle. Dipping his toes in the lower echelons of public service was not a bad visual. Why else would he be Deputy Head of the Department? At twenty-five? Again, Edith was happy it was not Walerian but his assistant who read her reports.

Walerian moved at a brisk step. The heels of his caramel Oxfords almost bounced off the floor. Edith noticed the conspicuous baby blue socks between the shining shoe-leather and trousers; her eyes ran up, searched frantically the space that separated the lapels of his suit jacket…there it was. The socks matched Walerian's cashmere sweater. It was something people gossiped about in the office, how the socks and sweater always matched. There was no reason for it, but Edith felt terribly angry at those socks all of a sudden.

And just as suddenly, Walerian was gone. In a heartbeat, his ridiculous twentieth-century, Arian-loving-fairy-tale look, blond quiff and taper haircut, crossed the corridor, went down the stairs, and out the building without his usual entourage. Something was going on. He looked preoccupied. His greyish-brown eyes flickered a couple of times, probably trying to find fault in what someone was doing so he could tell them off, have a quick release, thought Edith, but either there was nothing to latch on to, or he was genuinely too worried about leaving that he didn't notice. Is this about me? Did he read the report? Don't be ridiculous, Edith told herself.

As soon as Walerian left the Department went back to normal. Edith walked to the railing that flanked the corridor on one side, pressed her palms against the cold metal, and regretted it at once when she felt the sticky oiliness left there by thousands of passing hands. She leaned on her forearms instead, stared at the quadrangle around which the Department had been built, the old husk of Ms Hiu's home, the domed skylight and the greenery on the ground floor. It was like an ancient Spanish cloister, with the reception area in the middle, surrounded by offices and corridors. I should get that Water™ from the canteen. Or maybe Coffee™? I don't know. A buzz probably won't help now. Stick to Water™, she thought.

The bluish-white beam of the Khrónoloop towered at the centre of the quadrangle, from the ground floor to just a few metres below the domed skylight. The Loop was enclosed in a column of bulletproof glass, not so much to protect the Loop as to make sure that any Detritus did not go astray, to stop unauthorised personnel from putting things in the Loop, and yes, to protect *others* from the Loop, because no one fully understood how it worked. It stood at an angle, not like the tower of Pisa, but it did give the impression of toppling over unless righted by some giant hand. Like a spectacular tree, buzzing (not figuratively either, there was always a buzz around the Loop, like a neon sign on the roof of a motel...) with the secret energies of time. Edith saw a book pop out of the beam, hit the glass and fall all the way down to the ground floor, to the Basement collection area.

There was much scholarly debate on whether the beam was whitish-blue or bluish-white, but whatever the experts said, Edith had settled on blueish-white. The discovery of the Loop was an accident and had now become something of a myth. Grace Hiu, a socialite who joined the March of the Elephant Man, decided to donate her property in Neo-Pretoria to build orphanages, hospices, and hospitals. When the renovations on this building began and the workers removed the robin egg blue tiles in one of the bathrooms, they started hammering into the shower wall, and discovered that the noise

Ms Hiu had attributed to creaky pipework, a rusty, constant *whooooo,* like rushing water or an introverted ghost, was in fact a tubular beam of bluish-white light: the Khrónoloop, the Circle of Time. You can deposit an object inside, and someone will find it at some other point in time. Time is circular, we think, not linear. The problem is no one is around long enough to see the full circle, muttered Edith, repeating the mantra of every Khrónosemiotician. The Department of Khrónographic Affairs was founded shortly after the discovery of the Loop. Khrónography became a field of research. The government purchased Ms Hiu's townhouse and reconfigured and expanded the building into government facilities and office spaces surrounding the Loop. Heaven knows what became of those poor orphans.

What are you doing?

Edith turned. It was Conrad, smiling, something green stuck to his left incisor, jacket folded over his forearm. Not much, right? said Edith. Just going to the canteen. You? Coming or going?

Heading out. Late lunch with Norman and Gallaway. We're

going to The Lamp. They have specials on Tuesdays. Upstairs isn't happy with the Elephant Man going away in a puff of smoke, so, you know. Conrad scratched the side of his nose.

Oh. So what do they want you to do? asked Edith.

I don't know. They want us to come up with 'options'. To what? No one's sure. The guy disappeared and took his followers with him. Options? What options? It makes no sense. What solutions are there? Honestly, as much as everyone bitched about Ganeshiya, I think they were happier knowing where he was. Now nothing, *nada*. Anyway, it's not all going to be work. We probably won't work at all. Want to come? He paused, Hey, did you see Walerian storm out?

Edith shook her head. Don't know what that was about, don't wanna know, she smiled, and added, Wish I could come with you. Need to get back to work. Just a short break now.

Dr Crossman? May I have a word?

That was Saul Avery, Walerian's assistant, standing behind Conrad. Not as bad as Walerian, but still, most likely, another entitled brat from St Hubert's. Thankfully, Edith didn't have to deal with him often. Or not in person. Just electronically,

when she sent her reports, and with those he was quite efficient, actually. She had spoken to Avery once or twice, pleas-
antries, nothing of substance. Walerian had brought him into
the Department after becoming Deputy Director. Good old
nepotism. While Conrad was going on about The Lamp and
Gallaway and the Elephant Man, Edith had seen Avery turn
a corner and step into the corridor. It took him a few steps
to reach them. If Avery wanted to talk to her, that probably
meant he had read her report. Right? Shit. It's about Hell. My
interpretation. My lack of one. He noticed. Of course he noticed, thought Edith.

Certainly. I'm sorry, Conrad. Can we catch up later? she
said. Enjoy lunch.

Avery was taller than Edith. Bald, thin lips, the slightest
trace of a five o'clock shadow, even though it was only past
two. He wore a light grey suit: wool. Double-breasted jacket,
peaked lapels, pleated pants. Red tie with a double Windsor.
Rare these days for someone to wear a three-piece suit, but he
pulled it off. The lights from the ceiling shone off his scalp,
black, smooth like a freshly boiled egg. I called your office a

second ago. Lucky I ran into you, said Avery.

I am sorry. I had to step out. I need Water™, replied Edith.

May I walk with you?

Of course.

They reached the stairs at the end of the corridor. You were not born in Neo-Pretoria, were you, Dr Crossman?

That was a bit too personal a question to start the conversation, wasn't it? she thought. You can tell from my accent? I wasn't, sir. Or did you read my file?

Avery laughed, quietly, inwardly almost. Not your file. You have a very neutral accent. Hard to tell where you are from. But I know it's not local.

Edith was used to this conversation. She'd had it so many times she no longer found it tiring. It was expected, like introducing herself. Just what you did. Well, that's the thing. Everyone can tell I'm not local. Maybe I have a global accent. I don't know. I'm from Israel. A little kibbutz in the Jezreel Valley called Ein Dor.

Endor?

No. That's my accent again. It's pronounced *Ein* Dor. Anyway, I was born there. We moved to Japan when I was a little girl. My father's work. We left before the annexation of Kyushu and settled in Neo-Pretoria. So I have an accent in four languages, including my native tongue. Doesn't matter where I go, I'm not local.

Avery smiled. I see. By the way, I read your report on your translation of that new text, Dr Crossman.

They entered the canteen. It was full in spite of the late hour. Cutlery clanking, conversations bouncing off the walls. Edith was thankful for the noise. It gave her a few seconds to compose herself after Avery mentioned the report and her stomach felt like she had swallowed a cement sandwich. She paid for her Water™. Avery bought a Coffee™. What did you think? she asked.

It may be best if we discuss this elsewhere? It was not a question, but Avery had the elegance of phrasing it like one. He was, Edith started to think, very different from Walerian. Or was that his game? Maybe he is *more* sadistic and likes luring victims with a false sense of security, then goes for the kill. Maybe I'm about to get fired? Or maybe I'm being a psycho.

Stop jumping the gun. What if he has a gun? Stop it!

They took the elevator to Avery's office. That was quick. I had just sent you the report, said Edith.

It was a quiet morning, replied Avery. We're here.

Avery's office was larger than Edith's, but small for the standards of the Department. It was an appendage to Walerian's office with a door connecting the two rooms. Thankfully, the door to Walerian's office was closed. Even though Walerian was not there, Edith felt better with something between her and the place where he spent his time at work.

Opposite the door to Walerian's office, on the right-hand wall, there was a whiteboard. An inbuilt closet or cupboard stood next to it. Avery opened the closet door. He brought out a hanger, took off his jacket. Please, take a seat, he said, gesturing at the chair in front of his desk, which again, was quite small, only a writing desk. Your report. It reads…reluctant. What am I saying? You are reserved about your conclusions. Very tentative. Well, there are no conclusions, Dr Crossman, which is unusual for you. Why is that? said Avery. He sat down across the desk from Edith.

She put her bottle of Water™ on the desk. Translation is not a science, sir. It is an act of interpretation. Sorry to get technical and sound like a typical academic, *but,* there is no such thing as a 'perfect' translation. We knew that long ago, when we were translating *horizontally*, across geographical distance, across languages. Now that we translate *vertically*, across time, in particular texts from the future that reach us from the Loop, like this one, it is even harder. Unless there is incontestable evidence, and there rarely is, the best we can offer is an educated, informed hypothesis. Edith closed her eyes. Shook her head. But no, you are right. I am justifying myself. I struggled with my interpretation. I am not happy with it.

Thank you, Dr. I thought as much. Why is that?

Well, it was a difficult document to translate. The text is Neng, sorry, New English, which is tricky, said Edith.

Avery nodded.

You can tell by the substitution of certain phonemes for numerals, or shorter phonemes, like 'c' for 'see' and 'cn' for 'seen', or '2' for both 'too' and 'two', 'some1' instead of 'someone'. It is a direct consequence of chatspeak, and part of the process of contraction that many languages go through for practical reasons as they evolve. The 'g' in gerund endings is gone, so you end up with 'walkin' instead of 'walking', and not 'walkin'' with an apostrophe at the end, because apostrophes and quotation marks have completely disappeared by this stage. A number of words with 'be' drop the 'e'. We have 'bhind', 'bcome', 'mayb', 'b4' instead of 'before', but words like 'been' and 'below' stay the same, otherwise they would transform into 'ben' and 'blow', which makes no sense. 'Being' keeps the 'be' but drops the gerund 'g', and becomes 'bein'. That's the way evolution works: slowly, painfully, and sometimes arbitrarily when it comes to language. There are new contractions like 'xpensive', 'nxt'. The diagraph 'ck' drops the 'c' altogether, 'blak' for 'black', 'clok' for 'clock'. It seems that roughly two hundred years after the discovery of the Khrónoloop it becomes fashionable to say 'clock' instead of 'time', which later morphs into 'clocking' as an affectation, and eventually 'clokin', once the 'c' and 'g' are jettisoned. 'Th' is the most fascinating diagraph, in my opinion. My PhD had an entire chapter on 'th'! Sometimes it is reduced to a 'd' sound, 'dare' instead of 'there', 'da' instead of 'the', 'wid' and 'widout'. But just as often it becomes a 't', 'sometin' for 'something', 'tink' for 'think'. 'Through' becomes 'thru', and later 'tru'! It's incredible. But, I'm sorry, I digress, don't I? Of course I do! I always go down strange rabbit holes no one cares about, except me. Excuse me.

Edith cleared her throat.

Anyway, there's that and any number of other linguistic oddities, which are beside the point. These features of the language are a bit tricky but manageable. But the most troubling thing is Hell. The author, Silvius, says Hell is real. Ok, we can discard that one, sure. But given the style, and other texts I have read by him, I *know* it is an allegory. This is what worries me. What does it mean? I don't need to tell you, sir, in the past the cost of ignoring or misinterpreting texts from the Loop have been dire. The Australian famine, the collapse of the banking system, the monopolization of renewable energy. You name it. The list goes on and on. What type of threat are we talking about? I have no idea. That's the problem. Or, there is the chance that Silvius got tired, decided to write pure fiction, no allegories, and I am reading too much into this.

Avery kept nodding. We'll come back to that in a second, Dr, Hell as an allegory and how factual the text is. But the Holy House of the Charging Bull. What do you make of it? Your report barely touches on them, said Avery. He had a sip of his Coffee™, which Edith took as a cue to drink her Water™.

Well, I don't know who they are. It is the first time I have come across them in a Khrónotext. A new Dynasty, possibly? The text is far enough into the future that a new Dynasty could have developed? I am not sure, sir. I can speculate till the cows come home, but it's anyone's guess. Mercenaries, maybe, who want to become legitimate by establishing a Dynasty? It will happen, a few times.

Or an existing Dynasty that changes its name? asked Avery.

Sure. That is the other option. It would be unusual. As you know, Houses claim seniority through both longevity and capital. Changing a House's name is not quite like going back to square one, but close, said Edith.

Do you remember what the text says about the coat of arms of the Holy House of the Charging Bull? Avery stood up, walked to the whiteboard by his closet. He picked up a blue marker and took off the lid.

I remember what I wrote in my report, said Edith. The bull's head is front facing, surrounded by a circle. Its horns twist outward, symmetrically, to join the upper half of the circle, she added. As Edith spoke, Avery started sketching on the whiteboard. It looks like the horns grow out, then downward and become the circle. A suggestion of something? The bull becomes the world? Saves it? I am not sure. No other part of the bull shows, only its head. That's it, well done, sir. There is no motto, no shield, nothing. The drawing on the whiteboard was crude but similar to what Edith had described.

Avery put the lid back on the marker. Have you seen anything like it? he asked.

Well, no. That is why I cannot relate it to the existing Dynasties. The Seventeen are well known. The text says the Holy House of the Charging Bull strikes a diplomatic relationship with Hell, they become allies. A major Dynasty with the resources of a nation. So the Holy House of the Charging Bull, whoever they may be, *have* to be one of the biggest Houses of its time. Enormous. Which is why the text is so confusing.

Houses like that don't sprout out of thin air. They take hundreds of years. Millenia? That's why they become Dynastic. There should be some trace of them, but there is nothing.

Avery picked up the Coffee™ cup from his desk and gave it another sip. Have you ever been inside Walerian's office, Dr?

Everyone referred to Lord Walerian as 'Walerian', but hearing the name used like that by someone so close to him sounded almost like an insult. I haven't, no, said Edith.

Let's take a look, replied Avery.

I, sir, I'm not sure... mumbled Edith.

Don't worry. He won't be back for another hour or so. There is a crisis at home. Lady Patricia's surrogate is about to give birth to Walerian's new baby sister, the one to inherit the Mantle of the Oostanen Dynasty. It is going to take a while. We have until four thirty-seven, to be precise. Avery crossed the room and opened the door to Walerian's office. He stepped in. Edith took a few hesitant steps to join him.

The office was not the obscene mausoleum to Walerian's ego Edith had expected. It was much bigger than Avery's, but not ostentatious. A writing desk with a swivel chair. To the left, a filing cabinet pushed against the wall. On the opposite end of the room there was a tattered, green corduroy sofa, which shone like fresh moss when light from the window hit one of the arms. A rectangular table stood in the centre of the room, for meetings presumably, with a cream-coloured Formica top. Walerian's desk was in order. Not a pen, pencil or post-it out of place, no recently shuffled paperwork. Avery stepped behind the desk, opened a drawer. What do you make of this, Dr Crossman?

He was gesturing at whatever was in the drawer, which Edith couldn't see from her side of the desk. I feel very uncomfortable. Sorry, I should probably go, said Edith. She turned and walked a few steps back to the door that led to Avery's office. How does Avery know what has or has not happened to Lady Patricia's baby? she wondered. That's weird.

We are not touching anything. *You* most certainly are not. Only looking. I go into Walerian's desk all the time for work. Besides, this was on display for a very long time. When we were kids at St Hubert's, a good fifteen years ago, Walerian used to sneak us into his father's study when his Lordship Christian

Walerian II was away. He *loved* showing it off. Come, Dr. Take a look.

Edith stopped at the threshold between the two offices. Her senses were heightened. She felt like an insect, antennae up, primed for predators. How was Avery so sure Walerian was not going to come back and rush through the door any second? How could he know that? She walked back, stepped around the desk. Edith stared at the office's main door, waiting for it to open, obliterating her career. Then her eyes flicked to the open drawer.

A ledger. Leather. Burgundy, shoehorned into the tight space, it seemed, because there was no room between it and the drawer's walls. On it, a silver lighter. What is this? said Edith. Her actual thought was, Why on Earth are you showing me this, at the risk of losing my job? but she didn't voice it.

Daddy Walerian kept it in a glass cabinet in his study. It had its own spotlight and everything. A family heirloom. Even though Walerian was not allowed to go in his father's study alone, to say nothing of taking us with him, he couldn't resist. He *adored* lording the family history over us. The lighter belonged to Alastair Walerian, founding father of the House of Walerian. Market wizard and visionary. Take a closer look, Dr.

Gazes left no fingerprints. The lighter was rectangular with hard corners. The smooth silver, slightly reflective, well polished, mirrored the room around Edith and Avery with only slight warps. There was an engraving at the centre of the lighter. It broke the reflection of the room. The escutcheon of the Holy House of the Charging Bull.

Let's go back to my office, Dr, said Avery.

He closed the drawer, followed Edith out of the room and shut the door behind them.

This makes no sense, said Edith. What on Earth is going on? What has Walerian got to do with the Charging Bull? The Walerians adopted the hand-fan crest. This is well documented. The Japanese *mon* emblem, a variation of the Tang Dynasty, I believe, said Edith. That was Alastair Walerian's choice when he founded the House.

Dr Crossman, please. Is there a better-known logo than the Walerian's hand fan? We all use Mon currency. And is there a single person on the planet with access to credit who doesn't spend money on a Walerian product or service? Every day? You think I don't know this? I went to school with Walerian. As I said, he is *not* modest about family history. Why do you think we call him Walerian, and not Edward, or Ecgberht? This is Alastair Walerian's only surviving artefact. A relic.

Edith sat down again. She took her Water™ bottle from the desk, unscrewed the lid and drank what was left. I don't understand. So it is the Walerians who strike the alliance with… with Hell? They become the Holy House of the Charging Bull?

It is more complicated than that, Dr, said Avery. He walked back to the whiteboard. In his story, Silvius writes that Hell is empty. Not because Hell has sent its troops to conquer us or anything along those lines, but because there is no need for Hell anymore. When Silvius writes this, we, Earth, have become a place of punishment. There is no difference between us and Hell. *That's* what the allegory is about. Now, how does it happen? *That's* the key.

Forgive me, sir. So your…hypothesis, when Christian Walerian dies and Walerian assumes the Mantle, Edward Walerian I mean, he will change the name of the Dynasty to the Holy

House of the Charging Bull? And turn the planet on its head? All this is based on a lighter? Again, forgive me, but that is a stretch, sir. The Walerians are powerful but not invincible. There is still the Council of the Seventeen, at least another fifteen Dynasties to oppose him, if we assume the Oostansens will side with him, and there is no guarantee of that. I mean no disrespect. But there is no causal relationship here, nothing connects the dots. This is why Khrónotranslation is always tentative when we interpret a text from the future. It is *so* tempting to see what we wish to see. You have no proof, no silver string connecting the lighter in Lord Walerian's office and what you propose. What if someone steals the lighter in ten, fifteen years? Someone obsessed with the Walerians? And *that* prompts the naming of a new House? Maybe there are more lighters like that? Where did it come from? Why did it get that engraving? Our databases are good, but they are not exhaustive, and the world is a big place. Symbols have stories we don't know. Have you done the research? Not to mention, only I have read the original Khróno-text, which is locked in my office. You read my report, that's it, and there is no mention there of Hell being empty. You are correct, but you couldn't possibly know this. Edith's thoughts went back to her office. She *had* locked the door on her way out, hadn't she?

The evil that Silvius describes, what turns Earth into a living Hell, it's called Hypermercantilism. A new political and financial system. Unstoppable. Based on some of Alastair Walerian's most radical ideas. The Seventeen Dynasties end up ruling the planet. They monopolise everything. Get rid of the competition. They are bound by one person, a leader supreme amongst them. It starts with Walerian in that office, the future Plutocrat-Apostle. But there is a movement to oppose them. Chronologically, if chronology makes any sense when you talk in circular time, Silvius is the first of the movement. There are others, though. The Opposition. What would you say, Dr Crossman, if I told you that things other than documents can travel through the Loop?

What has that got to do with it? thought Edith. I would say this is not new, Mr Avery. The Detritus of the Loop comes in all kinds of artefacts. Primarily texts, documents, which is what *we* focus on, but anything inanimate and small enough to fit in the beam can travel across time, said Edith. Why? Do you think…the lighter? You think it is a Khróno artefact?

Avery snorted. That took Edith aback. That was unlike him. Far from it. The lighter is not the basis of my hypothesis on the Walerians and the rise of the Holy House of the Charging Bull. It is confirmation. This is more important than the lighter. What if I told you time travel is possible, Dr?

I would say you are a bit late to the party, Mr Avery. We are *always* travelling through time. The problem is we can only go in one direction, and at one speed. Unless you're an artefact dropped in the beam of the Khrónoloop.

You are funny. I mean, of course, what if I told you *people* can use the Khrónoloop? Not just objects. That you can even learn to calibrate 'when' you travel to? It is not random.

I would say, no. We, academics that is, have been speculating about this long before I started my doctorate. Much to our shame, we don't understand how the Loop works. That is why the documents that wash up on our shores from the river of time, so to speak, the famous Detritus, have been the focus of research, but whether the river of time flows forward or backward is still a mystery; directionality itself is not something we have proved. We don't even know where to start looking for the workings of the Loop. How to send objects to a specific temporal location? Who knows? So far there is no way of tracking or directing an object's time travel. *When* do they come from? Unless it is stated in the document, is very hard to tell. Which is, of course, what I do, the point of Khrónotranslation, to determine whether a text comes from the past or the future, and to interpret its meaning *contextually*. It is about understanding cultures that have not yet developed, sir. Carbon dating is useless because the texts have not aged; they have travelled through time, so they are as old or as new as when they were inserted in the Loop's beam. Even when a friendly pen from the future or the past decides to include a date in the document, you can never be sure whether that is reliable or not. Context is key. But anyway, to say that *people* can use the Loop, and even direct their travel? You know this is not possible. The Department is fully aware.

This is the point of no return, muttered Avery, like he was having a side conversation. I need to show you something, Dr.

Please, come with me.

Where are we going? asked Edith.

The Basement. To the Beam. I need to show you this.

They left Avery's office, took the elevator down to the ground floor. Its doors opened onto the quadrangle, with the Loop at the centre, a fountain of light that emerged from the floor tiles to the domed glass ceiling. The main elevator did not go to the Basement, which was a restricted area, under surveillance. Edith and Avery had to cross the quadrangle to take a second elevator, on the opposite side.

There was fake grass surrounding the Loop's base, artificial ferns and rhododendrons arranged to hide the tarp that fell from the ground level of the Department to the Basement, like a curtain, but working more like a toboggan that caught the Detritus and let it slide safely to collection bins, where it was sorted by expert handlers. The area was under twenty-four hour haptic, video, audio, and thermal surveillance. What Khrónographers *did* know about the Loop, early on, was that no segment was more or less important than the rest. In a *quantifiable* sense, infinity was contained within the Loop;

the 'space' of the Loop, the length, breadth, and width of the beam, were inseparable from time. But different segments of the Loop appeared and disappeared in different places at different times. This one, the Neo-Pretoria section, had lasted the longest. Other segments had been sighted for shorter periods, in Old Amsterdam, Alexandria, and Queensland. But again, no one understood the temperament of the Loop. Why it appeared in some places instead of others? How long the beam would last for? These questions remained unanswered.

Edith followed Avery into the elevator that led to the Basement. After the biometric scans they entered the collection area, which was pretty unimpressive. A rectangular room. On the left wall, there were shelves from floor to ceiling where the Detritus was categorised. The shelves were half filled with books, pieces of paper, vellum, papyrus; nothing big, no incunabula. Data storage systems, like USBs in plastic rectangles or squares, could now be decoded thanks to advances in museography. Glass pyramids, prisms, or spheres full of liquid also arrived every now and again, but if those too were data storage systems, the technology to eavesdrop on their secrets had not been developed yet. On the right wall stacks of empty plastic crates waited to be filled by the new Detritus after it was categorised on the shelves. A rotator belt circled the bottom of the Loop in the centre of the room. It wasn't moving.

None of this was new to Edith. The annoying buzz of the Loop and its beautiful, bluish-white glow, the two handlers sitting on chairs, talking, waiting for the Detritus to arrive. She was down here often, called in at least once a day to sort out future texts from past.

The handlers stood up when Edith and Avery entered the room but they continued chatting. Avery greeted them with a nod. May we have the room? he asked. As he had done before, at the canteen, it was an order, but Avery had the courtesy of framing it like a request. We will only be a moment. A minute, I should say. If you don't mind waiting outside. Thank you.

They were left alone.

Place an object in the beam for more than ten seconds and it will disappear. *When* will it reappear? No one knows. Past or present? No idea, thought Edith. She walked to the empty rotator belt, stretched her arm over it, and ran her fingers across the beam. She felt nothing, of course, no change in temperature, texture, or density. Because we never feel anything, do we, she thought, as we move through time? She pulled away. What was it you wished to show me, sir? Avery was smiling at her, fondly, like she was a little girl playing in the backyard and he was her proud uncle. It was creepy. Sir?

Avery searched the inside pockets of his jacket. There was something in his hand, a black, plastic rectangle. It *is*, the Walerians, Dr Crossman. The Holy House of the Charging Bull. The breaching of the Phnom Penh Convention, the union of the Oostanen and Walerian Dynasties into a new, unstoppable power. No question. There will be fratricide. Upon Lady Patricia's death Walerian becomes regent of the Oostanen Dynasty, supposedly until his sister comes of age. But then she doesn't. She dies, mysteriously. There is no legal provision for that, only a void that must be filled, by the only living Oostanen scion. They are going to bring the whole thing down. Well, Edward is. With his blindness, hatred, conceit, stupidity, ambition, and vast, self-perpetuating fortune. And the minotaurs. Bloody things! He is the start of Hypermercantilism. He opens the gates of Hell, figuratively, and everything rushes out. We can't stop it. The pendulum of history slows down, but if you hit it, it sways back stronger. The story has to run its course. But we can learn from it. *And*, we resist them. There needs to be an opposing force. That's how the story goes.

What minotaurs? Avery sounded like a zealot. That's exactly what he was. Edith was trapped with a madman, she realised. He kept giving her that eerie smile, the leer of the deranged. Avery looked at his watch. Almost time, he said. He held the black rectangle up, like a gun, like he was about to shoot a flare. Or worse. Bomb?

He pressed it.

Edith waited, her stomach turned to granite. *Was* it a bomb? Nothing happened. Was there a delay in the explosion? Surely security was on its way, the Orbs would have caught... she turned left and right, spotted each of the eight Orbs in the room. Their recording lights were off.

Was that you? You disabled them? How? Mr Avery, this is illegal. You know this is a felony. This part of the building is under surveillance at all times. What are you doing?

Avery was not doing anything. He was smiling. His hand went down one side, to the outer pocket of his jacket, where he put the remote control. He flicked his chin, raised his eyebrows, pointing to the centre of the room.

Edith did not know you could be too surprised to gasp. But there she was, not only speechless, *gaspless*. Surprise snuffed out by surprise.

It was a shoe. Black, leather, with a low heel, an ankle boot with buttons going up the bridge of the foot…and that was the problem. That was the extraordinary thing about an otherwise unremarkable shoe. It had a foot inside. And that foot was attached to a leg, which Edith could only partly see, because as the figure stepped out of the Loop's beam its purple robe draped downward, hiding the leg.

A woman had come out of the Loop. We can use the Loop, thought Edith. How? Did Khrónosemiotics get it right? How? Time travel is possible. How how how?

Avery crossed the room. He held the woman's left hand to help her step over the rotator belt. With her right hand, the woman held on to a long walking stick, a staff. Her hair was white, short, a buzz cut, like down growing on the round head of a hatchling. She wore sparse jewellery: a gold bracelet on each wrist, gold button earrings, and a round medallion with an elephant inside. Dr Crossman, said Avery. I did not *stop* the recording. I stopped everything. We are in a bubble. Same place, different time. None of this is being recorded. Nothing to worry about. Now, allow me to introduce you: this is the infamous Time Hag, Translator and Necromancer, the Witch of Endor. As far as we know, at least at this stage, the only person capable of travelling through time.

The woman laughed. Her teeth were young, pristine, her smile made her face wrinkle. We've met, said the Time Witch, and like Avery she smiled at Edith with unmerited tenderness.

Holy fuck, whispered Edith.

Another chuckle from the witch. There was a filled-in molar, Edith noticed, at the back of the woman's mouth, top left. Of course there is, thought Edith. The witch was slim, tall. Almost as tall as Avery, and taller than Edith in those boots. Old. Edith studied the woman's pixieish features, the strong cheekbones, the angular face. Black eyes like stretched almonds.

Pointy ears and chin. Of course they'd met. Of course. Edith had seen that face, the triangular scar above the left eyebrow, every day for the last thirty-six years.

Dear colleague of Archives and Records,

The following document is a transcription of Khróno-text #7396636, sourced from the official Detritus of the Khrónoloop. This untranslated, original text is in Neng (New English). A full translation has been submitted to the Deputy Head of the Department of Khrónographic Affairs, Lord Walerian, accompanied by my report of the same. I attach the present document for your records. Should you have any queries, please do not hesitate to contact me.

Dr Edith Crossman

Head of Khróno-Translation

Da Train

U only get 1 chance 2 c ur loved 1s again. I mean widout dyin, of course. Its not easy 2 get on Da Train 2 Da Land of da Departed. Da tikets r xpensive & hard 2 come by. Even if u can afford it, & u r able 2 find a real Witch 2 buy ur tiket from – Witches r da only 1s who can sell tikets, & Witches r rapidly bcomin xtinct – da Primitive eTexts say its a dangerous journey. U must go 2 Hell. Dats where da train leaves from, & few know how 2 make it 2 Hell in da 1st place. Dats why now Im walkin down da empty concourse. Da light filterin tru da glass ceiling reflected on da marble floor & columns is strong, so bright its painful, until a half cloud takes pity on me & filters da sun. I can c better now.

Dare is no need 2 line up at da counters, of course. I bought my tiket days ago, at great cost. Bsides, dare is no line 2 speak of. Da empty, open lunettes of da counters have no tiket sellers inside. Day stare out into da concourse like creamy, glassy eyes. I xpected dis, so Im not taken abak.

I keep walkin. I had imagined my steps would echo loudly in dis space, catedral like, & its so strange 2 hear day dont. Da hard sole of my shoe strikes da marble floor but I swear, by da muffled sound it produces, u would tink da veined surface is a rug, a carpet, not recrystallised carbonate minerals.

Dare is only 1 platform at da station. I know dis is where I should go coz da Witch gave me strict instructions when I bought da tiket. Da platform has no name: no letters or numbers 2 identify it. I guess it doesnt need 2 b distinguished from odars when dare r no more platforms at da station, right? As soon as I open da metal door leadin from da concourse 2 da platform I c how full its, burstin, it seems, wid a host of noisy creatures. Which creature will b my guide 2 da underworld?

Dare is no room in da platform, but I squeeze in. My chest is pressed against da flank of a grey bison. I feel da coarse fibres of my shirt, creamy off-white like old milk, brush my nipples. It hurts. Da shirt is homespun. My wife isnt very good at weavin. Now a blue snake, slim as a pen, slidders btween my feet. Im grateful Im wearin long pants, blue, & Ive tuked dem inside my boots so my feet r safe. I hear caklin & brayin, barkin. None of dose sounds could b heard b4 at da platform. Dare is human language 2, laughter, words I havent heard b4. A woman wid da head of a turtle stands nxt 2 a pillar smokin a long cigarette, her breasts bare 2 da sky.

Dare is a train waitin. I dont know how long its; as far as I can tell its as long as da platform itself, but I dont know how long da platform is eider, coz da crowd of creatures in front of me blok da view. But I can c someting approachin. A small animal. A peacok jumps on da bisons bak openin its quills, but dats not it, dats not da creature I was referrin 2. Da peacok coos. Its quills have 1000 ogles. I cant c anyting past dem. Wid anoder *coo!* it jumps off da bison. But now Ive lost dat odar creature I was talkin about. A racoon? A possum? Who knows, it probably wasnt headin my way, anyway. Cant c it anymore.

So I stand & wait. I was right. A creature *had* been headin my way. Now it stands by my feet. It gives da bison a kik in da bak leg, Move it, sister, it says. We got stuff to do!

A kat. Its coat is grey, so dark it looks like a fresh bruise. After da kik da bison walks away from us. Widout lookin up at me, da kat says, You know who I am, right? They explained it to you?

I nod, & I immediately tink dats stupid coz, as I said, da kat isnt lookin at me, but dat doesnt seem 2 matter. He speaks in Old World. It sounds so nice. Da way he rounds his '2' into 'to', & da fuller echo of 'you' instead of 'u'. As my teachers used 2 say, u *can* tell da difference btween our 'day' & his curly 'they', even dough we can no longer pronounce it.

Good. I'm Psychopomp, he says, but you can call me Psychopomp. Or the Wise Grey Cat. Whatever. Come on. I don't get paid by the hour so we better get going.

Da odar creatures on da platform disappear, slowly. Day bcome transparent as day continue 2 move & whisper & coo, until day r no longer dare. Psychopomp & I r da only 1s left. There you go, he says. I'm your perfect match. Strange, isn't it? No one ever expects their Guide to look the way they do. What do you know? Step into the train. The sooner we're done, the better.

What cart?

Silvius, it's empty. Whatever cart you want. It doesn't matter. The seats are a pain in the ass in no figurative way. You get the same stale biscuits and weak tea wherever you end up sitting. Martha the Evil Waitress will frown and try to trick you. You'll feel homesick as we travel from one Plane to the next. There is no First, Business, or Economy. It's all one class and it's all shit. So for once in this journey, lead the way, buddy. It's not going to happen again.

Half da words he uses make no sense 2 me, but I tink I get da idea. I dont choose da door closest 2 us, but da nxt, 2 da left. We walk in & da only remarkable ting is dat dis is da most unremarkable train Ive cn in my life. Da seats r covered in fabric, a faded, multicolored upholstery, ripped at da bak rest & bottom edges, yellow styrofoam pokin out.

Psychopomp jumps on a seat, Come, sit in front of me, not by my side. That's it. You and I need to be facing each other. I will face the direction the train is moving in, and you'll face the opposite direction, back to the station, all the time. Listen to me carefully, you can never, *never* look forward on our way there. Your eyes need to be looking *opposite* the direction the train is going in. Get it? *Away* from Hell. You need to be looking back. All the time.

I struggle wid his accent, but I tink I understand what he is tryin 2 say.

So just be obedient and look at my face as we head there, ok?

I obey Psychopomp, sit down & look str8 ahead of me, which means bak in da direction of da station. Im a big fan of Gluk, an Old World, Pre-Drought composer. Nobody knows about him any more. We studied him when I was a student at da Concertatorium. I recorded 1 of his arias. From da opera *Orfeus & Eurydice*, but my manager convinced me not 2 release it wid my 1st album. Dis was b4 Moder got sik, when da world was a nice, plump, juicy oyster, & I was ready 2 press da shell 2 my lips. I was a decorated war hero wid a beautiful voice & looks dat not only a moder could love. Anyting more romantic dan dat? Producers were trowin contracts at me like da Papacy trew bombshells at us during da Great Drought War. I was booked 4 da musical capitals of da world: Aukland, da Principality of Guatemala, Austin, London. Good times. Did Orfeus look bak as he was rowin der barge out of Hell? Or Eurydice? I cant memry.

Da train ride is smoot, again, surprisingly unremarkable. I dont know how long it will take us 2 get dare, & even if I did, I dont tink conventional clokin applies here. At da end of da aisle Im facin, bhind Psychopomp, dare is a door. It opens, & a lady walks in pushin a trolley. She wears a striped shirt, a uniform most likely, an apron tied around da waist dat stops me from cin weder she has a skirt or pants. She is overweight, not dangerously but considerably. Da way she pushes dat trolley u would tink its a walker. Her strides r short & wide, wid a pendular sway from side 2 side, like a windup toy, only slower. Short, curly hair, faded blonde; no bonnet aldough dat wouldve been a nice touch. She has 2 warts on her face, 1 on da bottom of da left cheek, facin me, 1 opposite, close 2 da cheekbone. Like confused nipples. She stops nxt 2 us & I c her hips r wider dan da trolley. She *is* wearin pants, blak, like da apron.

Any*thing*, duckies? she asks, wid an Old World accent, stress on da -*ing*, like Psychopomps. Her smile is tired, a habit, not da fruit of a well of joy gurglin in her chest. I've got nice tea, and lemon bickies, she says.

We'll pass, Martha. Thanks. Just give us Safe Passage, replies Psychopomp.

Martas face turns hot pink. Her eyes dart from side 2 side. Da sad, sweet lady who had been pushin da trolley is gone, or rader, she is still dare, but someting has changed. She looks like a zooed animal, her face is a cage, & whatever is zooed inside is desperate 2 get out, peerin from bhind her eyes, fat iron bars. Sure you don't want anyth*ing*? A macaroon? she asks.

I said Safe Passage Martha, thanks. Psychopomps tone is bored, pedantic.

Marta reaches into her trolley, under a tray, & drops 2 squares of plastic on our table. Widout anodar word she resumes her walk down da aisle. I cant turn my head 2 c what shes doin, but 2 judge by da sound I tink she leaves tru da door bhind me. I stare at da squares of blue plastic on da table.

She's not nice, says Psychompomp. He liks da bak of his

paw. Someone tricked her into this job when she was on her way to The Train of the Departed, like you, God knows how many eons ago. She'll get out if someone eats or drinks what she offers, but then the poor sap she tricks will have to take her place until some other fool bites. It's never a good gig, but she's *so bad* at it! Even if I wasn't here to protect you, honestly, would you have tried any of that stuff? Of course not! But hey, she's got the Safe Passages, right, and we can't get anywhere without those, he laughs pointin wid his nose at da blue plastic squares. Condoms! he screams.

Im confused. Da word must b Pre-Global, coz I dont recognise it, What r condomoms? & what is Safe Passage? I ask.

*Con*doms. It's not cardamom. They are something from Martha's time. Never mind. It's just a crass joke. Who did you see when you bought your ticket? Brianna? She's terrible. She never explains anyth*ing*! Who was your Witch? asks Psychopomp, wid a similar pronunciation 2 Martas.

Edit...

From Endor? Did she wear a big, round medallion with an Elephant on it?

I nod.

Really? That's strange. Edith is usually very good. Meticulous. Did she give you the Incantation to call me, in case you are in trouble? asks Psychopomp.

I nod; she did, but I cant memry da exact words.

Oh good. At least there's that. Anyway, we need the *condoms* for Safe Passage, to get in and out. Otherwise you always end up having trouble at the border, and you don't want that, especially on your way out.

But, do we, wear da condomoms? How does it work?

No, you duffus! You don't… Never mind. The shape of the Safe Passage doesn't matter. That's something Martha came up with to embarrass you, cause she was annoyed. It could've been two thimbles or eyes of newt, or whatever. The important thing is to carry yours at all times. And I mean all times. I am no protection without it, ok? Even with it, things can get tough. Oh, we're here.

Da train slows. It doesnt take long 4 it 2 stop. Psychopomp takes 1 condomom & I take da odar. Alright, this is us. Let's go, he says. Chop chop, or we'll miss the other train, and that's the one you *really* want.

We walk out at anodar station, also empty. Across da platform, over da lintel of a doorway, is a wooden sign swayin lazily on 2 rusted hinges. It looks like da sign of a saloon, or a caricature of 1. Da words 'I endure eternally' r hand painted on it.

Our platform is on the other side of the station. Let's go, says Psychopomp.

I follow him. Sometimes, Psychompomp rears bak, standin on his hind legs. I get da illusion of bein wid a small furry human wid a funny face & not a purposeful animal. Da Neo-Catolics tell us dats precisely what we r not, dont day? We r not animals, but blong 2 a different order of creation; xcuse me, Creation, capitalised. Cin Psychopomp scurry away on all 4s reminds me of dat. Im no Neo-Catolic – I wouldnt b here if I were, now would I? – but I was brought up by a devoutly unanalytical fader, & a very nonchalant moder when it came 2 religion.

Dis station is also marble, wrought iron, & glass. I follow Psychopomp 2 da far end, where a pair of glass doors leads 2 our platform. He gets dare b4 me, wid enough clokin 2 run bak 2 me. We've got about forty-five human minutes until the train gets here. If you want to step out of the station and check out the Spiral, briefly, you can. You won't have time to make it to the Ninth Circle, so don't even try. You can probably see two Circles, at most, said Psychopomp.

Will u come wid me?

Nah, I've seen it too many times. I'll stay here and rest. It's not what it used to be, but if you haven't seen it before, it's worth checking it out. And keep your Safe Passage safe, in your pocket or close to your heart or whatever. One of Virgil's great ideas. Nothing can hurt you while you have it with you, except maybe an Officer, but that's it. Haven't seen one of them in eons. Don't lose it. Remember: you lose it, you're cactus. And if you're late, you're cactus too. Outside the station doors you'll see a huuuge tree, a cypress. That's Laurel. Wave hello from me, will ya?

I dont know what a 'cactus' is (was?) but I nod a couple of clokins. I tink Psychopomp smiles, but its hard 2 tell widout lips. I turn & head 4 da main doors of da station. I walk out.

Da 1st ting I c is da tree, like Psychopomp said I would. U cant miss it. Enourmous. A wide base of curlin roots flow in every direction like da waves of a river. Den da branches bcome da sky. I walk past it, wavin. Psychopomp says *hello*! I say. No reaction. I feel stupid.

After da tree I find myself in a village. A town. Da place is beautiful. Like dose reconstructions of archaic towns across Eyurope, whose names have been lost 2 war or clokin. Da streets r cobbled, every roof is tatched wid tiles of beautiful colours. Tulips & geraniums sit outside da windows. Da town isnt very big. In a few minutes I make it 2 da centre, a tall, walled citadel atop a hill surrounded by sturdy, broad walls. Da citadel isnt 2 big eider. I circle its wall, count 7 gates, all loked.

Da town is empty. Not a soul in sight. But its not abandoned, tings havent gone 2 seed. Everyting is trimmed, swept, no overgrown weeds anywhere. Its just empty, like dare was a big festival happenin somewhere else, & every1 had gone dare. I keep walkin.

Da point where dis part of da Spiral finishes & da 2nd Circle of Hell bgins, is very clear. Da light dims, noticeably.

Not a glimmer or glare. It isnt pitch blak, I can c, but dare is no brightness. B4 me is a gently slopin valley dat again, not surprisingly, is empty. At da end of da valley I can c da 3rd Circle. Its not 2 far. I start walkin in dat direction. Its cold, & annoyingly windy. I walk past a group of boulders, arranged in a circle, like a nest. In da centre sits an enormous, translucent, papery ting, flappin in da wind, like a tent, or da sail of a ship. Its not paper, I c when I step closer. Its da shed skin of some enormous snake. I know Im protected wid da Safe Passage, so Im not scared, but an unpleasant feelin does take over me. Da silhouette of each scale is about da size of my head. Da name 'Minos' is etched on every1. I keep movin.

I tought I was goin 2 make it 2 da 3rd Circle, but I cant. I only make it as far as da border of da 2nd. Its rainin in da 3rd Circle, a str8, dense curtain of liquid dat marks da limit of da border. What stops me from goin dare is da smell. Whatever is fallin down from da sky, its not water. Im curious 2 c what lies ahead, but not dat curious. I hear tunder, trice split, a strange clap, & den realise its not tunder. I cover my nose 2 avoid da smell, strain my eyes past da sheets of fallin, liquefied putrefaction dat pass 4 rain here. I can c a figure lyin on da ground. Its big, da size of a small house, wid tree very long neks. Id say da neks are da longest part of its body. Day end in wolves heads, or someting canine, snarly. Da monster is asleep, on its bak, tree tongues loll out relaxedly btween sharp teet. Its got no fur as far as I can c. Blak skin, which makes it difficult to c parts of it in da poor light. Da legs are splayed. I cannot c its genitals, so mayb it has none, or day are hidden in da shadows. Its snorin. Dats what da tunder is, its snores.

Anodar tundery snore, which probably my cue 2 leave. Dont wanna miss da train. But den I hear someting else, different from da stinky drone of da rain. A shout? Greetin? I still cant c anyting tru da storm & I cant tell where dat noise comes from, if my imagination didnt make it up. At 1st its hard 2 tell, but den 1 of da shadows bcomes more solid, darker dan da rest, & I c a figure, antropomorfic if not human, approachin.

It *is* human. Male. Old-Caucasian. Overgrown brambly beard. His clodes r ancient. Da pattern of da weave on his over shirt is new to me. He wears a red loop, a ribbon of infinity on his nek, below da chin.

There! Can you see me? he calls out again.

I stop & wait 4 him, I can, yes. Hello! I raise my shoulders 4 a formal hello. He seems confused.

My name is David, he says, when he's by my side. He raises his arm, holdin da palm of his hand in front of him. After a few seconds he brings it down again.

Were u in da 3rd Circle? I ask. How did u manage 2 enter da 2nd? I tought u were confined 2 ur assigned Section?

No, I am not in Glutony, he replies. Further down, considerably. One of the last Evil Ditches, the Malebolge, which are all the way down to the Eighth Circle. And you are right, it used to be that you could not move, but all the Officers and Guardians are either asleep or gone, like this one here, he points at da snorin, tree-headed monster close by. On my way here I didn't see Geryon, or Plutus. I have no idea where they are. I think I may be the only one left. I really don't know. It is hard to tell. So I just keep exploring the place, he says.

What happened? I ask, Why da emptiness?

Excuse me? he asks.

Why da emptiness, I repeat.

Oh, *the* emptiness, you mean. Apologies, I could not hear you, he says.

I tink he could, but he has trouble wid my accent, like I wid his.

David shrugs. Again, I do not know. I think with time, we just became irrelevant. Obsolete. You need to be able to keep up, modernise, and the things they were doing to us here were no match for what we humans do Pre-Departure. *That* is Hell. See, I stole a book from a great library, fooled a trusted friend to do it. My greed and arrogance got the best of me. *The Hypermarket* was an important book, historically. Still, it was not like I stole, I do not know, the cure to Hedgehog Influenza or cancer. I still think that what I did was minor. But I ended up in the Seventh Bolgia any way, the Eighth Circle. Our punishment was to be bitten by snakes and lizards all the time, until we burst into flames, then came back from the ashes, like a phoenix of torture, and then it all started again. Of course it was painful, but you get used to it. You stop feeling after the fire, and I never minded reptiles. I used to have a pet iguana, Galland. The gentleman chained next to me in the Malebolge was a herpetologist. Similar story. He was in pain, but he just could not pull his eyes away from those snakes. He was fascinated by them. There was nothing like that on Earth, of course. So it wasn't *that* much of a punishment for him either, compared to what could happen to us in the world nowadays say, if you forget to pay a bill. At least those were the last reports I got. Have you heard of the Cashiers? Those minotaur things? Are they before or after your time? He shudders, Evil lot. The Holy House of the Charging Bull is unforgiving. What can you expect, though, if it was founded on the murder of Beatriz Oostanen by her brother Edward. But I digress. I think the Boss here was tired, too. One day he just quit, and here we are.

I honestly dont know what 2 say. Half da words he uses make no sense 2 me. His English is Pre-Global, 2 archaic, even older dan Psychopomps. I got da word Cashiers, of course I did. Felt nauseous. Dressed in blak, da white circles on dare shirts. Da Chargin Bull always lookin at u from inside dat circle. Horns spirallin, twistin out. Dose horns r da spirals of Hell.

I purse my lips 2 show David Im takin him seriously. Im

very sorry, but I gotta go. I need 2 catch Da Train 2…

David interrupts me. Oh, that is why you are here! Of course. They still do The Train of the Departed? So you can see your loved ones? We used to have visitors like you often, back in the day. No, I understand. Of course. You *do not* want to miss your ride!

I dont. Tank u. It was enlightenin 2 meet u, David.

Thank you. What's your name?

Silvius Rivera.

A pleasure.

Can I ask, David, b4 I go? What r u wearin? Whats da meanin of da lemniscate around ur nek? Were u part of an order? & ur over-shirt. Ive never cn a textile like dat!

David looks confused 4 a moment, den he laughs. I cannot blieve da mans rudeness, but I suffer it stoically. No, this is called tweed, he says. The fabric. We used to call them jackets. Good in winters where I lived, Boston. Well, near Boston. I don't know what it's called in your time. The thing on my neck is a bowtie. A sign of formality and respect to others. It happens to look like the lemniscate, I suppose, I never saw it that way, but nothing to do with infinity I am afraid. It was nice to meet you, Silvius. Now run, before your train leaves.

I jog. I no longer run after dat bullet grazed my right hip, when I was fightin 4 da Roman Horse in da Great Drought War. My joggin still works, even wearin boots. I make it bak tru da windy valley of da 2nd Circle in what feels like no clokin, & halfway down da empty city I slow down 2 catch my breat. Safer not 2 run on cobblestones. Past da cypress, I can c da station only a couple of steps away.

I reach da double-glass doors at da station, push dem. Day dont budge. I pull. No difference. Is dis da wrong set of doors? I turn, look at my surroundins. No, dis is definitely it.

Panic from stomach 2 toes. I feel it in da bak of my knees 2, weak, acidic. Psychopomp! Help! What is da Incantation 2 call him? What did da Witch say? I shouldve written down da words! I need dem. I need his help…

What r u doin?

I turn around. Dare is a woman in uniform bhind me. Her skin pale. Pasty. She has tried 2 remedy it wid makeup, but its badly done. Da line of makeup finishes under da jaw & da rest of da nek is a different tone. I can c da veins in her underarms, light blue, like her short sleeved shirt. Blak pants & shoes, blak leader belt. A cap of blak blue; strands of strawberry blonde hair escape from it.

U know da rules. Go bak, she says.

Oh, tank u. No. Xcuse me. Dare has been a mistake. Im not meant 2 b here. I need 2 take a train dat will depart soon. My guide, Psychopomp, is byond dose doors.

I take a few steps bak, & now she is standin at an angle, btween me & da glass doors. She seems offended by my presence. Dats what I read in her xpression. Her face looks like a mask tryin 2 hide fear, or anger, or outrage. I dont know. Only da eyes show dare is some1 dare, & day r fixed on me.

U need 2 step bak, she says.

Wait, no. Ive a pass. Ive Safe Passage, I dig inside my pokets 4 da condomom. Da panic dat blossomed in my stomach b4 flowers again when I find my left poket empty, den da right. I catch my breat again when I feel soft plastic. Dare. Psychopomp gave me Safe Passage, I say. Well, he got it 4 da 2 of us, c?

I step 4ward. Pain grips my arms. Im torn from inside. Da pain is in my legs 2, my ears. My body knows its interconnections & everyting is a reflection of everyting else & everyting hurts. I cant yelp, coz Im frozen by pain.

U cannot approach me, sir. I told u 2 go bak. What u say makes no sense. Dis isnt Safe Passage. I dont know what dis is. U r not movin until I know what Circle u blong 2.

Im goin 2 miss da train. Dis is it. I will never c Moder again. Deat, real Deat, has finally caught up wid us, as day always say it does.

I hear tappin, knokin. I c Psychopomp on da odar side of da glass doors, gesturin at me, den at da woman. He is moutin someting but da sound is muffled by da glass. Da woman is lookin at him 2, but she wont approach da doors. She wont leave her post. Someting cliks & da glass doors open, & Psychopomp stumbles out. We're going to miss the train, Silvius! What are you doing?

Evidently, I cant answer. Im on my knees now, still in da grip of what Blonde has done 2 me.

Officer, excuse me, Mr Rivera and I need to catch a train.

We cannot miss it. Our documents are in order, we are merely transiting. He is not meant to be here. He is not a Resident. See the Safe Passage in his hand? Psychopomp shows his own Safe Passage. I have one too. They were legally obtained on the Entry Train. We have the legal right to leave on The Train of the Departed if we so wish.

Blonde stares at Psychopomp widout sayin anyting. She blinks. Ive never cn a Safe Passage like dis. I need confirmation. Her accent is closer to mine dan Psychopomps or Davids. Da tings we notice in da middle of a crisis.

Martha's humour. Wretched wretch. As you know, I wouldn't be able to be here if I did not have legal, bona fide documents. Please, see for yourself. Perhaps you have not inspected my friend's, out of caution, of course, understandably. But do examine mine and you'll see. Psychopomp holds out da blue plastic square.

On da floor & step bak, she says, leave it on da floor. Psychopomp does as he is told. His blue plastic square lies btween dem.

Da pain is no longer dare. I dont know if Blonde turned

it off, or if it just ran its course. Im still numb, conscious but numb, & all I can do is collapse on da floor, like Psychopomps dropped condomom.

Blonde xtends her arm. Da condomom floats 2 her hand. Dare is a shimmer around it, a bronze halo dat pulses twice & disappears. Den she turns 2 me. Ive already dropped my condomom, unintendedly. She repeats da process wid mine, da blue plastic flies 2 her hand & glows bronze.

Ure clear. Blonde looks at me. U r blokin da Exit. U need 2 move, she says.

Psychopomp comes 2 my rescue. Thank you. We'll be leaving now, he says to Blonde. Come, Silvius, we've taken enough of the Officer's time. Let's go. I feel his paw xplore da bak of my nek, palpate left & right until it settles on a spot at da base of my kranium. He pushes. Da numbness & pain in my body r gone. Psychopomp bites my shirt & drags me across da floor, past da glass doors, into da station. Da kat is remarkably strong.

Tank u, Psychopomp. Dat was…I dont even know what…

Move it! Train! Now!

He scurries away & I follow him. Psychopomp is 2 fast 4

his muscle mass. Clearly, Fysics makes xceptions 4 him. I do my best, run as fast as I can. Dis is da last chance 2 c my Mum. If I dont catch Da Train of Da Departed…dats it, never again. I memry her hands, so small & skinny, wid da oblong nails painted bright red. Liver spots where tumb & wrist meet. Movin & active but so defenseless. How could dose hands fight after 70? She couldnt defend herself from da Cashiers. May I live long 2 slice deir troats open. Parents should never age. Day certainly shouldnt die. No 1 should ever die. Xcept da Cashiers. Love shouldnt finish. Why is da rule book so full of pain?

I *gotta* make dis train. I dont care. Ill fight a 1000 Blondies 2 get on it if Ive 2. Psychopomp is lightnin. He runs along da walls, over a sofa. Da doors 2 da platform r seconds away. Why did I go out? Dare was no need 2 xplore. Not when someting dis important was at stake. I shouldve stayed here, waitin. How stupid can I b? U just dont risk it when its someting dis important. U dont. Da glass doors r perfectly transparent. I can c da train. Is it movin? Red lights r shinin, blurred halos. But is da train movin? I dont know. I cant tell from here. I need 2 c my moder 1 more clokin. Dont do dis, wait. U havent left yet, have u?

Wait 4 me.

The Rise of the Holy House
of the Charging Bull

The stone walls groaned with the shake, and a quiet drizzle of sand and pebbles fell on Theodosius' forehead. He dropped two rolls of papyrus out of the armful he was carrying. If the Serapeum was shaking, their tectonic defences had been breached, which meant he had little time before the army of the Charging Bull stormed in.

He crouched to pick up the rolls, hoping that another geoblast would not make him lose his footing. It didn't. When he was down, instead of picking up the rolls, he let the armful he was carrying drop gently on the floor's stone slab. There was no time to lose. And yet. If they were all going to go soon, he may as well see what was happening, thought Theodosius. Such is the inconsistency of the human heart. We don't always do what we are meant to.

Briskly, he walked up the stairwell at the end of the corridor, to the roof. It was only one level up, so it should not take long, he told himself. He only wanted a glimpse. And wasn't that morbid? A glimpse of his friends' defeat, the most definitive failure of the Opposition. But it was History too, written in the stylus of time right before his eyes. And this was his calling. Good or bad, moral or immoral, he was going to watch.

The ramparts of the Serapeum were alone, as Theodosius knew they would be. The battle was taking place outside the walls of the building, beyond the force field that dug deep into the Serapeum's foundations and reached up to its highest drone, and was their last line of defence. If the geoblasts were making the building shake, that meant there was a battering mole somewhere, underground. They didn't have much time.

Beyond the walls of the Serapeum, the armies of the Charging Bull were weaving death blows with the Opposition's forces. Ganeshiya was on the ground, as always, at the forefront of his followers, stomping his feet left and right, turning neutrino daggers into grass. There was a gash on his forehead, orange blood pouring out like lava. The wounds of a semigod. By his feet, wherever the Wise Grey Cat hissed, death followed. But even this was not enough. The armies of the Plutocrat-Apostle were overwhelming. Ferocious minotaurs that felt no pain. They swarmed the city and port. Alexandria was a hive, a boiling cauldron of the soldiers of the Holy House of the Charging Bull. Theodosius felt a nervous tremor of emotion, an unpleasant emptiness on the back of his knees. Before the siege he had never witnessed a battle. His gladiatorial arena was limited to scrolls, and the sharpness of sentences, and the way meaning fought its way in translation as it breached the borders of a language to conquer the next.

Theodosius scurried down the staircase, back to the corridor. For a second he thought his scrolls were missing and he felt a pang in his stomach, but then he found them, exactly where he had left them. He ran to the heart of the building where his commanders were waiting.

The Serapeum had been under siege for close to thirteen months. The Plutocrat- Apostle's forces came from the sea. At first they were held back by the Elephant Man, but eventually the army of the Holy House of the Charging Bull overwhelmed them, as Theodosius and everyone else had known they would. Still, Alexandria had the resources to resist for those thirteen months, if not as the only remaining stronghold of the Opposition, at least as the last one to openly resist the rule of the self-named Plutocrat-Apostle Walerian III, reigning Prince of the Holy House of the Charging Bull. Plus, they had the Witch's Army.

Which was useful, but not invincible. In the end, the walls fell. The Plutocrat-Apostle's minotaurs burned Alexandria to a crisp. Edith's Incantations helped slow them down for three weeks, but there are reasons why the inevitable is labelled thus. They all ended up in the Serapeum, an offshoot of the Library of Alexandria, where the Khrónotexts were stored. Theodosius inhaled deeply again: yes, the final stronghold of the Opposition.

The room where the Time Witch had gathered her forces was not big for the standards of Alexandrian architecture. There were two tapestries on the walls, a dozen folding chairs for the Witch's Privy Council, with soft leather seats arranged in a circle at the centre. Thirty-seven wooden statues surrounded the room, effigies of Gods, humans or both, with removable limbs and heads that were used as storage chests for the papyrus scrolls.

Some of the chairs were empty. Ganeshiya was still out, of course, fortifying the forecourt and keeping the minotaurs at bay. CloudMan was never present, locked away in his tower, but a seat was reserved for him out of courtesy. Saul was there, sitting to the Time Hag's left, his hairy legs spread widely to allow his genitals to rest on the leather seat. Since the Battle of Abu Qir, when Saul's legs were reduced to mushy stumps by the neutrino blade of a particularly sadistic Bull soldier, the Time Hag had used Language to give him a new set of legs, which turned out to be goat legs, but no less useful. Silvius, like many of their friends, had fallen in battle, but his seat, like those of the other fallen Council members, remained present. Laurel was there too, half woman, half Cypress. They kept

talking as Theodosius unscrewed the head of a crocodile stat-
ue on the far side of the room and put away the armful of
papyri, all but one. Yes, they would all be gone soon, so putting
the papyri away was useless, but *the principle* was what mattered.
And damn it, as the Witch often said, the moment you lose
those principles the other side wins. Everything goes to rot.
When he took a seat to join the circle, everyone went silent.
Theodosius rested his hands on his knees, looked around.

Sorry, Giver, said Edith. It's not you. We were just talking
about the future, which is grim as we all know. We've known
for a long time. It doesn't make it easier, does it? 'Giver' was
what the Time Witch called Theodosius. It came from the et-
ymology of his name, Giving to God: Theos=God, Dosis=-
Giving. So Theodosius was the Giver. He didn't like it, not
particularly, but there you have it. Edith rested the Lance on
her thighs and started fiddling with her medallion, the round
one with Ganeshiya's emblem inside. How did you go with that
translation? she asked.

She knew how he'd gone with the translation. She'd read
it, in the future, but Edith never allowed chronology to get

in the way of manners. Well, I think. It's finished, the whole diary. Until the part where the Aunt's village burns down. It's scary. I'm glad I won't be here for it. He regretted the words the moment he said them. Laurel, they knew, would be present, witness to the rise of Hypermercantilism. In tree form, but present and no less aware. She was staring at the ground, bark for skin, with twigs here and there, roots burrowing from her toes into the stone floor, but other than that, mostly anthropomorphic, unperturbed, it seemed, by Theodosius' comment.

Good. Or bad. In any case, it means we are ready. As ready as we are going to be. The tremors are becoming more and more frequent, which means Ganeshiya won't be able to hold off the geoblasts for too long. As soon as the Loop flashes, Giver, you drop in your translation. That's it, folks. We need to close the circle. There's no other way. Laurel, time to face the bull-y, my dear, said the Time Witch. God, she may be going down, but she just won't let go of that wretched sense of humour, will she? thought Theodosius.

Avery can stay and help me, she added. I'm nervous. We all know how it ends, but still. Doesn't make it any easier, does it?

No one answered. Theodosius tried to smile but it was a half-smile. Out of politeness. The whole thing felt anticlimactic.

They're here, said Laurel. The Elephant Man has fallen back. My root systems on that side of the building are burnt. The Bulls want us alive. They're sending a squadron.

Of course they do. Avery, hold the book, please, said the Time Witch.

Her Lance rasped the floor, close to the sole of her left ankle boot. Edith of Endor was the only person Theodosius knew who refused to wear sandals in this weather. She started unscrewing the Lance at the middle.

Theodosius had finished translating the last part of the text. Of course, once the circle was formed, terms like 'first' and 'last' would become useless. The Khrónoloop was the story that made time circular. The discovery came about with Edith Crossman's research in Khrónosemiotics, which, as it turned out, she plagiarised from the Time Witch herself. But because Crossman and the Time Witch happened to be the same person no one was terribly concerned about the ethical implications of the problem.

As Crossman's research pointed out, every language is sequential. One letter, or grapheme or cipher follows the next to build words, which in turn form ideas, expressions, and so forth. From beginning to end, always, sequentially. It doesn't matter if we read right to left, left to right, top to bottom or the inverse, the process is always *linear*. The question that drove Khrónolinguists mad for decades was whether our use of language was a consequence of the properties of the spacetime continuum, a forward, one-way street, or if we experienced the spacetime continuum as linear *because* of the way we used language. In other words, pardoning the expression, did language determine how we experienced time, and for that matter, reality? The Scribes were still asking themselves these questions when Theodosius attended the Prince's school. They were the theories *du jour* in the Wisdom Texts, even though French had not yet been invented.

And then the Time Witch appeared, tapped him on the shoulder to join the Opposition, and answered his questions. Turned reality inside out when she showed him the Loop. The past is a memory, the future a hypothesis, she claimed. The present is the eternal grindstone where they meet. And linearity exists only because of language. When we escape the linearity of language, we escape the linearity of time. Human awareness is the object with a centre of gravity strong enough to bend time, given the right linguistic code. And that new code, the language that punctures reality, is what Edith Crossman dedicated her life to develop, with a bit of help from her future self. A code that could render the spacetime continuum malleable. The Khrónoloop. Simplistic minds would call it magic.

The time had come to get the whole thing started, to create the Khrónoloop, to say the words out loud and give the Opposition a chance, even if it was a chance to hide and bide their time. Hypermercantilism was the perfect trap. For all his pettiness, Edward Ecgberht Walerian, First Patrician of the Holy House of the Charing Bull, Supreme Commander of Capital Forces, Plutocrat-Apostle, was about to consolidate an almost perfect system. Perfect for the Plutocracy, of course. Prior to Hypermercantilism, the Seventeen Dynasties controlled the Earth's resources. To an extent, they balanced the playing field, keeping checks on each other as allies and enemies, undermining the former and partnering with the latter. With his claim to the Mantle of two Dynasties and his minotaur army, Edward Walerian was able to join the other Dynasties under his banner. The self-perpetuating idea of a natural, organic market structure, Market Reality: thus is the way of the world, this is how it has always been, and it will continue to be. Nothing to discuss, folks, nothing to question. Keep buying.

Avery and I will take the Loop, once it is formed, said the Time Witch. Giver, remember, your translation has to survive the fire, to make it to the diary of Nándor Custos-Hora. Ganeshiya will be fine. Amerintha will be born soon, Empress of her Race. My brother Peter is safe in his tower. Laurel, the next five thousand years as a tree, until you face Phoebus again. The seeds are sown, dear friends. Time it is.

Saul Avery stood up, away from the folding chair. His hooves clicked on the stone floor as he crossed the room. He opened one of the statues, a man-sized owl whose breast was hinged on each side to allow for cabinet doors. He brought out a book, unusual these days with the resurging fashion of scrolls. A large, blue incunabula with no title on the spine or anywhere else for that matter. Or at least not a title Theodosius could read. Edith had assured them the word was there, in her new language of space and time, but she was the only one who could read *Khrónoloop* on the leather cover.

Saul's hooves clicked back to the circle of folding chairs. Edith raised her right arm, pointing one of her wands to the sky, the Past; the top of her robe slid, exposing her breasts. Enjoy the show, Jacob van Oostansen, old pervert, she muttered. The second wand, the Future, was firmly planted on the ground. Saul opened the book.

History. Again. Theodosius was about to witness the beginning. Of course, the word 'beginning' supposes the existence of linear time, and within the syntax of the Khrónoloop, past present and future exist together, so the meaning of these words implodes. Still.

The ground shook. Whether that was a geoblast or the start of Edith's incantation, Theodosius had no idea. A two-headed owl poked out from the side of the Witch's skirt. It moved its head in a semi-circle, sweeping the length of the room with its gaze. Behind Laurel's folding chair a goat began to graze on the floor. There was nothing to graze on the naked stone, but the goat did not seem to mind. Four tentacles wiggled out of its head. One of them held on to Laurel's chair and let go almost immediately. The Time Witch's words re-arranged reality, just as an editor would do to a sentence in need of a good re-write, like this one, perhaps. Theodosius heard a shriek. Above, in the darkness of the ceiling, where the glow of the solar candles almost couldn't reach, he saw a woman, naked, riding the skull of a leopard, pulled by two roosters. Her ginger locks as long as she was tall, trailed behind her like the tail of a comet.

Theodosius' eyes went back to Edith and Saul and he saw it for the first time, even though it wasn't the first time. A bluish-white glow. In the chaos of the moment, Theodosius did not notice the buzz, but it was there too. Either there was no time to lose or they finally had all the time in the world, all the world in their time. Who the fuck knew? You had to be Ganeshiya or the Time Hag to understand these things, or at least pretend that you did. Theodosius walked to Edith and Saul and dropped his fresh translation of *The Hypermarket* into the column of light between the Witch's wands.

Epilogue

Jacob Cornelisz van Oostsanen was cold. He wiggled in bed, trying not to wake up his wife Adriaentje. It was time to get up. He didn't want to. A few more minutes of warmth would do him no harm, would they?

Winters were for the young, and winters in Amsterdam were for the brave, and at fifty-six Jacob thought of himself as neither young nor brave. He had been living in Amsterdam for the last twenty-six years, fathered two sons there, bought his first house in the Kalverstraat, the busiest street in the city, and then the house next to it, but as his name indicated, Jacob was not from Amsterdam. There were some who called him Jacob Cornelisz *van Amsterdam*, but they were mistaken. He came from Oostzaan.

A tiny village in the North of Holland, East of the river Zaan, Oostzaan was a quiet place. Which is why he and his brother Cornelis decided to move to the city. There wasn't much work for painters in Oostzaan when they lived there. Ironically, which is how Life usually operates, most of his commissions over the last ten years—and some of his best works too—came from Egmond Abbey, also in North Holland, very close to his native Oostzaan. Partly funded by Lamoraal, Count of Egmont and Prince of Gavere, patriarch of one of the most powerful families in the Low Countries, the Abbey had deep pockets, and since that wretched Luther started spreading his schismatic nonsense, they were happy to invest heavily in images that kept the fold together. Blessed be Luther, thought Jacob.

He opened an eye. It seemed to be snowing outside. It was hard to tell without light. The eye closed again. Of late, the big commissions had dwindled, but Jacob ran a workshop with pupils, which included his sons Cornelis and Dirk. They designed stained glass windows, woodcuts, and book illustrations, and that still brought in more than enough to get by, and buy good bacon. It was Jacob's hope that Dirk and Cornelis would continue the family trade. Dirk eventually would, passing it on to his son, also Cornelis, but by the time Jacob's grandson's work would come to flower, Jacob himself would be long gone, his remains fertilising the more tangible, less abstract flowers of Oude Kerk Cemetery.

But now Egmond Abbey wanted a new painting. Blessed be. *God schept geen mond, of hij schept er ook brood!*, thought Jacob, and when he cackled with gratitude a cough took over and he felt Adriaentje stir by his side. He also felt his left lung singeing like the devil's flaming hand was giving it a good squeeze. Jacob worried constantly about his lungs. He thought death would come for him with pulmonary tuberculosis or pneumonia, some horrible, airless prison where he would suffocate to death. He shouldn't have worried. Death would come to him swiftly, in seven years' time to be precise, after slipping on the street trying to avoid a demented draft horse and hitting the back of his head against a stout cobblestone. But for now, Jacob sat up in bed and clutched at his nightgown, the spot above the sternum, which in his mind was the most vulnerable to the cold.

This time, for their commission, the masters at Egmond wanted something to inspire more fear than faith, an image to warn possible defectors from heading in Luther's direction. Well, *the* master of Egmond. The good Abbot of the Black Monks of St Benedict, head of Egmond Abbey, gave Jacob no more details. Normally this would not be a problem. But Inspiration, the wretched bitch, refused to visit. Jacob knew he was not an artist. He was a craftsman, a pretty good one. He got the job done in time. That's how he had made a name for himself and built a business. But there was always a spark, a hint, a mysterious catalyst playing on the back of his eyelids that showed him the way before he got started on a new work. This time, though, there was nothing.

Time for the plunge.

Jacob got out of bed. The most delicate hint of dawn had begun to colour the sky. There was snow but it was mild. With his foot he touched a cold spot on the floor, by his bed, until he felt his stockings, and sat on the edge of the bed to put them on. His robe should be on the floor too, where he dropped it last night before hopping into bed...but it wasn't.

Still on the edge of the bed, Jacob swiped the floor with his feet. There was no trace of his robe. Where in the name of Satan's bright gonads did he leave it? He always wore it before bed to avoid catching a chill, and it waited patiently until morning in the rumpled heap by his bedside. But there was nothing.

The other option, of course, was Adriaentje. Did she pick it up after he fell asleep? Didn't she fall asleep first? Jacob wasn't sure. In any event, if the robe was not by the bed it had to be in the wardrobe, and only Adriaentje could have put it there. Five, seven steps in the cold to the opposite end of the bedchamber. He could survive that. Of course he could.

Jacob's hand went back to his sternum, back to clutching the nightgown. He scurried toward the wardrobe as quietly as possible, trying not to wake up Adriaentje or slip to a prompt death on his stockinged feet. The wardrobe door creaked open, and there it was.

Not his robe, hanging by the nail on the door, as he expected to find it. All thoughts of the missing robe and hostile chill had vanished. And let me tell you, that took something when it came to Jacob. But what, exactly, did it take?

A bluish-light beam. A column of light planted before him. It buzzed like an army of drones that had come to fight him. Jacob tried to cry out, call Adriaentje, but he couldn't. His voice was gone. A gasp, a squeak, a chicken's indignant chirp when you kick it on the side. Was the column made of glass? Was it transparent? The strange colour, that pale blue, seemed to be hiding something.

Someone?

A woman, enrobed, not in Jacob's unaccounted-for nightly garment, but a purple mantle of sorts. Her breasts were bare. She held two sticks, one pointing at the floor, the other to the sky. Behind her there were ruins, a collapsed building, and beyond, a port, ships, an army like nothing Jacob had imagined was remotely possible, of men with bulls' heads. Sprites flew across the sky, witches and demons. A man with the face of an elephant. All manner of monstrous beings had been set loose in that beam.

Jacob slammed the wardrobe door. Adriaentje woke

up. What is it? she asked, her voice raspy but alert, the throat uncleared yet. What happened?

What happened, indeed? Jacob had no idea. In there, he said, pointing at the wardrobe, which was useless because there was not enough light for Adriaentje to see in the gloom, and even if there had been, she was embarrassingly short-sighted to begin with.

She was getting annoyed, What are you talking about? Is someone in the house? What happened?

No, Adriaentje! said Jacob. He was shaking now. His knees were moving sideways, and a shiver that had little to do with the cold had taken over his body. The wa-wa…, he stammered. I'm telling you! It's the wardrobe! Adriaentje!

Adriaentje got out of bed. She slapped her cheeks to wake up. Slowly, because there was still no light, she walked toward her husband. You are telling me nothing, Jacob. What in the name of bread and yeast are you talking about? I hope Anneke's already up, getting the oven going. What's in the wardrobe?

Jacob felt her standing next to him. Her hand found his,

then pushed forward to find the handle on the wardrobe door. Jacob hesitated. Adriaentje, it's...

But before he could finish the door was swung open. Jacob was slapped on the face, lightly–it was more a brush than a slap–by his robe, hanging from the nail on the door.